Guided Practice

Jamie Jones

ISBN-10: 1-947208-10-1

ISBN-13: 978-1-947208-10-0

2ND EDITION

A Note to the Reader

This edition of Guided Practice is a complete revision from the first edition. The original work was published in 2014.

CHAPTER ONE

WELCOME NEW HIRES the sign above the entrance screamed. A shudder ran through Lara Rumson's body as she made her way up the sidewalk, sweltering in the heat of a Louisiana summer. Surrounded by colorful balloons, bright banners, and smiling faces, the run-down old building obviously had been decorated in an attempt to spruce it up. It didn't look like a happy place. Chipped paint, dirty windows, faded awnings. Institutional and uninviting. She estimated it to be built in the 1950s. Vista Terrace Middle School, set deep into a neighborhood, needed some updating.

It appeared to be a middle-class neighborhood. Somewhat generic.

Lara took a deep breath, hoping they had some chilled bottled water for the new recruits. Although the air was not terribly humid, her clothes stuck to her as she approached the doorway.

A cherub-faced woman greeted her at the door and handed her a tote bag.

"Welcome!" The woman's broad smile stretched across her cheeks.

"Thank you."

It was orientation day for the Portsmith Independent School District, and they appeared to rolling out the red carpet. The district had a lot of vacancies, and Lara had landed a plum job here after working hard at her career. The thought of meeting her new principal made her stomach lurch. Lara had been hired directly by the new superintendent. Rather than promote from within, he'd gone over several principals' heads and hired directly from surrounding school districts. The locals didn't appreciate recruitment tactics that aggressive.

When Lara entered the office, her nose burned from the chemical odor of something. She couldn't quite discern it. A woman sat behind the desk, her hair glistening with some sort of product.

Perhaps that's what smells.

"Good morning, I'm Lara Rumson."

The woman looked up but didn't say anything.

"I'm here for the orientation."

"It's in the library."

"Where's the library?"

"Not so fast. Miss Hawthorne's gotta meet you first."

Lara tensed and clutched her handbag so hard her nails dug into her palm. Awkward didn't begin to describe her situation. She was about to meet her principal *after* she'd been hired. Highly irregular.

The woman gestured Lara to an open doorway in the rear of the office.

Here I go.

She approached the door, suddenly not feeling the air conditioning. Perspiration trickled down her forehead.

A stoic-looking woman sat behind a desk. Her head was down as she wrote something, so Lara knocked on the door. The woman looked up with a stiff smile. Her gaze appeared to go through Lara rather than at her.

"Come in. I've been expecting you."

Lara approached her and offered her hand. "I'm Lara Rumson."

"Claire Hawthorne. Your principal." Miss Hawthorne gestured for Lara to have a seat. "I see you've spent the past five years teaching in a neighboring school district. And now, you're my new vice-principal." The woman's gaze scanned Lara up and down, as though studying her.

"Yes, ma'am."

"Since I didn't have the benefit of interviewing you, I've been placed in the position of trusting Dr. Hamilton's judgment." Miss Hawthorne sat back in her chair. A heavyset woman, she wore a well-tailored suit and her hair in a bun. "You must have done something quite spectacular to impress him."

Lara smelled the condescending tone. "Dr. Hamilton saw my leadership presentation when I completed my master's degree program. He called me in for a meeting a short time after that and offered me a position here."

"That was very sweet of him."

An awkward silence. Lara wished she could escape from those eyes glaring at her. Her ears burned and her stomach fluttered.

"Bachelor's degree at Louisiana State, master's at Tech," Hawthorne read from a resume.

"Yes, ma'am."

Hawthorne lowered the resume and focused on Lara. "You've only taught five years. The minimum eligibility for an administrative position."

"I have the necessary certifications, ma'am."

Hawthorne let the resume drop to her desk. "Must have been a good five years."

Lara didn't respond. Her stomach tightened, and she gripped her handbag so tightly she feared the straps would snap.

"I run a tight ship, Ms. Rumson. There may be times when I have to call on you to be bad cop to my good cop. One thing I want to make clear is that you mustn't forget there's only one principal at Vista Terrace, and that's me. I make all the decisions. Nothing is done without my approval."

Lara nodded. "Yes, ma'am. I'm looking forward to working under someone with your experience."

"You should be, since you have no administrative experience of your own. But I'll take good care of you. You'll have nothing to worry about." Miss Hawthorne glanced toward the door. There was another young woman standing there, probably a teacher. Miss Hawthorne nodded to Lara. "You may go now."

Lara's legs wobbled as she slowly rose from the chair. With a steady stride toward the door, she was certain Miss Hawthorne's gaze hadn't shifted. Lara smiled sympathetically at the young woman waiting outside the door.

Poor thing.

"Oh, Ms. Rumson. One more thing." Miss Hawthorne's voice cut through her.

Lara turned to face her new principal.

Miss Hawthorne glanced down. "You'll need to wear more comfortable shoes."

"Ma'am?"

"I approve of how corporate you dress and you should look professional. However, as vice-principal, you're going to be running around this campus all day putting out fires. You may want to find something more comfortable to wear."

"Thank you." She hurried out of the office.

On the first day, she picks on my shoes?

"Is there a ladies' room?" Lara asked the office secretary.

The woman gestured to the hallway.

Rattled by the meeting, Lara slipped into the ladies' room and let the tears flow. Her hands trembled with rage.

How dare she.

Hawthorne behaved as though she were more important than the superintendent. The conversation she'd had at her interview came back to her. Hamilton had said there were a lot of old mindsets in Portsmith. Lara had just met one of them.

This woman resented her for being handpicked by Dr. Hamilton to be vice-principal in a school district where she hadn't taught. Miss Hawthorne probably looked at her — and any of Hamilton's picks — as the enemy. Lara splashed some cold water on her face and dried her eyes. She faced an uphill battle to prove herself. What a way to start the year.

If she planned on surviving here, she had to develop a strategy to not allow that woman to get under her skin. Lara tossed the towel in the trash and took a few deep breaths before heading out.

When she found the library, Lara grabbed a seat at a table with a couple of other strangers. Rummaging through the tote, she found a calendar, schedule, benefits guide, pens, pencils, sticky notes, a city guidebook, and some promotional flyers and coupons.

"What grade do you teach?" a woman seated at the table asked.

"I'm the new vice-principal. Lara Rumson." Lara extended her hand.

When Lara mentioned her position, the woman narrowed her eyes. She shook Lara's hand with merely a nod but didn't introduce herself.

Lara pretended to take an interest in her tote bag. Although the woman at the entrance had shouted *welcome*, Lara wasn't feeling it.

"Oh, yikes! Look who's here," a woman at the table purred. "That's Kelvin Young."

"Of *the* Young family?" another woman at the table asked.

The mention of his name sent a wave of nerves through her. Every part of her body tingled, and gooseflesh rose all over her. The Young family. They were a wealthy family of old money made in oil. Everyone for miles around knew the name. She was all too familiar with Kelvin from his pictures splashed all over social media.

In fact, it was hard to miss him.

Ladies' man. Man about town. Playboy. Man-whore. At least, that's how the gossip columns had played him. She couldn't recall seeing pictures of him doing anything more extraordinary than showing up at charity events.

Kelvin Young strutted across the room in crisp dress pants and a neatly pressed bright coral polo shirt. A broad frame filled his impeccably clean tight-fitting shirt, outlining each bulging muscle. Above average in height, he probably topped out at six foot even. His flawless raven complexion contrasted nicely with his attire.

Lara's core surged with heat. How could one man be so damned good-looking?

"He's the most eligible bachelor around." The woman sighed.

"He puts the up in uppity." The other woman's face soured.

"No way."

"Gotta be with all that money…"

"What's he doing here?"

Kelvin approached their table. "Is this seat taken?" His smoky voice like a smooth radio disc jockey, he could knock Barry White off the charts.

Shock waves reverberated through Lara's body. How could one voice have so much power?

"No, go right ahead. I'm Tierra." She grinned a bit too broadly.

"LaTasha," the other woman said quickly.

"Hi, my name's Kelvin."

His statuesque frame hovered above Lara. Wall-to-wall

muscles, the cut of them visible against the fabric of his clothing. A rush of warmth filled her head.

He took the seat next to Lara and met her gaze.

"Lara Rumson."

"It's a pleasure to meet you."

His large hand wrapped around hers. A jolt of excitement rushed up her arm. A handsome man, probably no more than thirty, with a strong jaw and captivating eyes. Better than merely handsome, he exuded charisma. Not difficult to imagine how he'd gained his reputation.

Trying to process the reaction she had to his touch, Lara neglected to reply.

"She's an ice queen," Tierra muttered to Kelvin.

Did she just refer to me as an ice queen?

"So, Kelvin. What are *you* doing here?" LaTasha scooted her chair closer.

Before Kelvin responded, Dr. Hamilton had approached the table.

"Miss Rumson, it's good to see you."

Lara rose and shook his hand. "Dr. Hamilton."

"Mr. Young, Miss Rumson, can I have a word with you? I won't take but a minute."

Hamilton gestured to a quiet corner of the library. Once they were out of earshot of the others, Hamilton spoke.

"You're both going to be strong additions to this district. There's a lot of more work we need to cover, but by hiring you two, I know we're off to a good start." He placed a hand on each of their shoulders, leaned in slightly, and dropped his tone to a near whisper. "You know this school's in bad shape. I'm counting on you to turn it around." He dropped his hands and resumed a normal tone. "I look forward to working with you. I'm off to another school now."

He shook both their hands again and headed for the door.

Lara spotted Miss Hawthorne in the doorway, her gaze squarely on Dr. Hamilton.

Trepidation loomed in the air. Hamilton had squeaked in on a seven-to-five vote, and the five dissenters were vehemently opposed to him. He'd already made sweeping changes in the hiring process, and school hadn't even started yet.

Hawthorne clearly wasn't happy. From their first brief meeting, it was obvious to Lara that Miss Hawthorne loved to call all the shots. And Hamilton's words were prophetic. He'd told Lara and Kelvin they'd been hired to turn Vista Terrace around.

Isn't that the principal's job?

Lara turned back to Kelvin, but he was gone.

Now where did he go?

When Lara returned to her table, she found it empty. The two ladies had joined another table, and Kelvin was nowhere in sight.

"Ms. Rumson, would you come here please?" Miss Hawthorne stood behind a counter with a couple of other people she hadn't met yet.

Lara grabbed her handbag and tote. "Yes, ma'am?"

"You're on my administrative team. You don't sit with the teachers—you stand with me."

"Yes, ma'am." Lara placed her handbag under the

counter and took a deep breath. This promised to be a learning experience for her, probably more so for her than for the students at Vista Terrace.

Someone handed Lara a blank name tag and a Sharpie. She nervously scribbled Rumson and slapped the nametag on her jacket. Another woman, whose nametag read Logan, had a shit-eating grin on her face as Lara stood next to her.

"I'm Miss Logan, the school counselor." The woman's clammy handshake was unsettling.

"Lara Rumson." She didn't feel the need to repeat her title after the reaction she'd gotten a few moments ago.

Lara shifted her weight from one four-inch heel to the other. A few more people drifted in. Glancing around the room, she couldn't spot any coffee or donuts. This was a cheap school and didn't feel welcoming at all.

"Can I have your attention please? We're about to get started."

Miss Hawthorne had a commanding voice. Almost instantly, the room fell quiet.

"Standing to my left is the newest member of my administrative team. Dr. Hamilton has gifted me with a new vice-principal. Her name is Ms. Rumson, and I look forward to seeing what she can do for Vista Terrace."

So now I've been gifted.

Miss Hawthorn went on to introduce some of the new teachers, but Lara tuned her out. Her gaze was fixed on the library doorway. More specifically, on the man who'd just entered through the doorway. It was Kelvin.

Lara's nipples swelled against her bra. She had no idea

why this was happening. Must be nerves. Starting a new job in a new school district.

Yeah, that's it.

The morning droned on uneventfully, with Miss Hawthorne laying down the law of the land. Lara gained a clearer picture of why the school had such low test scores. Hawthorne seemed awfully set in her ways. She clearly wasn't open to new staff, so she probably wasn't open-minded to new ideas, teaching strategies, etc. It had become apparent to Lara there was only one rule here—Miss Hawthorne's way or the highway.

My new principal hates me.

The look in Hawthorne's eyes when she'd seen Dr. Hamilton speaking with her and Kelvin could have cut glass. Lara had worked harder than ever on her administration certification so she could move up in rank, and now Hawthorne looked at her as though Lara were something stuck on the bottom of a shoe.

I earned that master's degree and I'm gonna use it.

After a couple of boring presentations, during which Hawthorne kept glancing at Lara—probably to see if she was paying attention—there finally came a break for lunch.

"Lunch is catered today, courtesy of our new superintendent. Enjoy it. We don't usually receive such amenities." Miss Hawthorne directed her gaze at Lara as she spoke.

A crew of workers from a local deli carried in a crate full of boxed lunches. There weren't too many new staff present. Miss Hawthorne supervised them as they loaded the boxes onto a table, then waited until they left the library.

"Ms. Rumson, please see that everyone gets fed." Hawthorne nodded and left.

Lara had a sinking feeling that she could do no right in Miss Hawthorne's eyes. As one of Hamilton's recruits, Lara would be scrutinized. Relentlessly.

As she passed by each table, she encouraged the new hires to proceed to the lunch table. When she reached Kelvin, he sat writing in a notebook.

"Get your lunch."

He didn't respond.

She placed her hand on his shoulder. "Mr. Young, don't you want lunch?"

Kelvin met her gaze with the most beautiful charcoal eyes. "Yes, ma'am." He smiled and gestured for her to go ahead of him.

**

Damn, she's gorgeous!

Her hips swayed from side to side as she walked ahead of him, long legs gliding elegantly in high-heeled shoes. She had shiny blond hair and emerald green eyes. A finely tailored business suit with a hip-hugging skirt and sharp jacket completed her image.

A bit aloof, though.

Actually, he preferred that to the two vultures who'd sat across the table earlier and looked like they wanted to devour him. That was a major turn-off. At least they hadn't stayed long. It didn't take much to rebuff a gold digger—the story of his life. Women either threw themselves at him or ignored him. No happy medium.

Ms. Rumson kept cool, but he could work on that. Despite her frosty demeanor, she was someone he wanted to get to know. He couldn't figure out why, but she intrigued him. Perhaps because she reminded him so much of a cool blonde from a Hitchcock movie.

In fact, she could have stepped out of a Hitchcock film. Her blond hair piled on top of her head like Tippi Hedren in *The Birds*. She had the allure of Eva Marie Saint in *North By Northwest*. Her cool, aloof demeanor reminded him of Kim Novak in *Vertigo*.

There was an extra skip in her step, accented by those curvy hips. Now that was something he wanted to grab and hold tight.

She's hot.

But he hadn't come to Portsmith ISD to flirt with women, so he'd better get her out of his head right now. Her striking beauty proved difficult to ignore. Something else that he found impossible to ignore—her touch.

She put her hand on my shoulder.

His whole body had jolted with excitement when she'd placed her hand on him. Although just a light tap, it'd generated intense heat.

Damn, what's her first name? Laura? That isn't how she said it, though.

Kelvin approached the lunch table. Turkey, ham, and chicken were the choices. He grabbed a turkey box and picked up a Coke from one of the ice chests set up by the table. When he returned to the table, Miss Rumson already sat with a boxed lunch and a Diet Coke.

Kelvin glanced down at her box. She'd chosen ham. This had been an awkward first day, and the principal barely acknowledged his existence.

Is she mad 'cause Hamilton hired me?

He made a mental note to fill out the application for the teachers' union that sat in his tote bag. He'd need all the help he could get in this district.

Kelvin focused on his lunch. Smoked turkey with provolone cheese and a choice of condiments, some potato chips, a cookie in the box, and of course, an apple for the teacher.

He looked over at his new vice-principal. "You need an aspirin yet?"

"For what?"

"First day tension."

"No, but thank you for asking."

"At least Hamilton's got our back." Kelvin opened his soda can.

Lara didn't respond to his comment.

"Excuse me." Lara rose and left the room. When her back was too him, she sucked in her breath.

Is something troubling her?

That cool, aloof exterior had cracked. Something must be on her mind.

Easy on the eyes, but more than good looks. She had class. Did he have to write her name down in ink on the palm of his hand so he wouldn't forget it?

Laura? Lara? Lora?

He wasn't doing so well with that today. It had better come to him if he wanted to get to know her.

I'll just call her Ms. Rumson.

One thing was certain about Ms. Rumson—there was more than met the eye. But what caused her to be so distant? Courteous and professional, clearly well mannered, but he could not call her warm. Could it be a front she put on since she was a vice-principal, or was it something more? A large part of the position, at least at his old school, dealt with discipline. Perhaps she put on a tough exterior to brace herself for the daily problems of combative middle school students.

We're in the same boat.

They'd both been handpicked by Dr. Hamilton, and Kelvin had an alliance with her that he likely wouldn't have with anyone else.

Does she feel the same for me?

Perhaps she couldn't. As vice-principal, she was above him in rank and hardly needed the support of a lowly teacher. He had a sinking feeling in his stomach that this year was going to be all about proving himself. After eight years of teaching, he still had doubts about his abilities to make a difference. Was he good enough? Did he get through to the students? Could he be strong enough to help them succeed?

Hopefully, his talents as a football coach and passion for teaching science would shine through.

At the next table sat another man. In fact, he was the only other male in the room. Kelvin found that odd. There should be more male role models at a middle school.

"Kelvin Young." He offered his hand.

"Randy Strode," the other man said before looking away. *Okay.*

"I teach science and coach football. I was recruited from the Niles School District, and I look forward to working here."

"Math and basketball coach." Strode didn't look up. His chiseled face hardened, and his tawny hue faded into his dull beige suit.

Short and not so sweet.

Kelvin left him alone and returned to his agenda. Fortunately, Hawthorne had allotted some time after lunch for teachers to work in their classrooms. What he wanted to do was spend time with the vice-principal.

One thing had already become clear. He and Ms. Rumson both had a major obstacle ahead of them—Miss Hawthorne. If they were going to institute the changes Dr. Hamilton outlined in his vision, one of two things had to happen. They needed to somehow convince Miss Hawthorne, which so far appeared unlikely. Or they had to go headfirst against her to fight for every change.

I'm up for the challenge.

"Attention. I need your attention, please." Miss Hawthorne came through the library door as though making an entrance from stage right.

"Your room assignments are on your schedules. You are dismissed to your rooms now. Be back here at two for a brief presentation."

As Kelvin got up from his seat, Randy Strode was at the lunch table helping himself to a second box. Kelvin glanced down at Strode's schedule. Two periods of sixth grade math, one period of seventh grade math, and a lot of blank space. He must be one of Hawthorne's picks. Hamilton's people were getting worked to death.

Kelvin walked down the hallway to his classroom. Paint peeled from the ceiling. The school was old and badly in need of a cleaning. The floors were dull and pieces of tile cracked. He reached his classroom, a depressing, musty place with a stale odor and a lack of any color.

Although he'd always worked with at-risk kids, he'd served them in a school with more modern amenities. Vista Terrace stood like a relic from the past.

"You have a lot of work to do, Mr. Young." Miss Hawthorne hovered in his doorway. "And only a couple of days to do it. I hope you're ready to work hard here at Vista Terrace."

"Yes, ma'am."

Miss Hawthorne nodded. If a nod could be described as curt, Miss Hawthorne's would qualify.

Did I make the right move?

CHAPTER TWO

Highland Heights, a section of a quiet suburb away from the city, served as Lara's home. When she unlocked the door to her condo, all she could think about was swallowing two aspirin. Today had been stressful. Tomorrow featured a full schedule of professional development, which meant she'd have to spend all day with Miss Hawthorne. She plopped the bottle of aspirin into her handbag.

When she placed her keys on the table, she glanced into the mirror.

Maybe I am an ice queen.

Those words from the new teacher today had sliced through her. She shook her head and turned away, gazing at her living room.

Lara's parents had invested wisely, and the condo had been a gift upon her graduation from college. She'd been overwhelmed by their generosity, but her parents lived a comfortable life and could afford it.

They'd done so much for her. Supported her through college and grad school. Been there for her every step of the way. If only she could do more for them. Express her gratitude. Her heart heavy with guilt, she sometimes questioned if she deserved to be so blessed.

Lara had worked her butt off to earn her two degrees.

But my new principal still hates me.

Lara had to earn Hawthorne's trust. Got that. Nothing came easy. Pulling her weight and more didn't intimidate Lara, and she could face the challenges ahead of her.

Mr. Young had made that comment about Hamilton having her back, but she didn't share his confidence. Hamilton had a job to do, as well, and he'd be overwhelmed with work. He wouldn't have time for petty nonsense between a principal and the new hires. And so far, Miss Hawthorne hadn't done anything unreasonable. She merely behaved like a cat pissing to mark its turf.

But that Mr. Young. Something about him stirred things inside her that had no business being stirred. She had zero interest in men right now, not after what had happened to her in her youth. Not even a man as drop-dead gorgeous as Kelvin could ignite a spark. Then again, a little eye candy wouldn't be so bad to distract from the headaches inflicted by Miss Hawthorne.

Damn, he's handsome.

He had a perfect complexion. Not a blemish or a line on his flawless, inky skin. His body was solid muscle. Kelvin clearly worked out.

Lara picked up one of her numerous paperback novels but couldn't focus on reading. Stretched out on the afghan her grandmother had knitted for her, she had hopes of drifting into a much-needed nap. But first, she'd need to push Kelvin out of her mind. That wouldn't be easy.

His winning smile. Broad shoulders. Warmth permeated her as she drifted off to sleep.

The next morning, Lara arrived at Vista Terrace wearing comfortable shoes. And just in time. Miss Hawthorne gave her a walking tour of most of the campus. It was every bit as old and creaky on the inside as it looked on the outside. No wonder Dr. Hamilton was doing so much to pump new blood into it. The tour concluded at a dingy, dark, windowless room.

"This is your office. Feel welcome to decorate it any way you wish."

Lara gazed at the room in stunned disbelief. Practically empty except for an old wooden desk and chair, plus a dented old rusty wastebasket. The walls barren. No signs at all that this was the previous vice-principal's office. From the stained and chipped industrial-looking sink in the corner, it could have been a custodial closet.

Miss Hawthorne handed her a thick ring of keys.

"Here they are. Book room, supply closet in the main office, your office, of course, and most of the other places I showed you. The gold key is a passkey to all the teachers' rooms."

Lara bit her lip. This wasn't the time to protest. Miss Hawthorne, and probably some of the other principals, likely had decided to make life hell for Dr. Hamilton's picks. Hardly in the best interest of the children, yet still part of the politics of public education. Lara found herself in a different school district and had to accept that things were different here. And other things, like petty bullshit, not so different at all.

"Thank you, Miss Hawthorne. I'll get busy setting up my office."

Miss Hawthorne nodded and began to walk away.

Lara let out a deep breath.

"Oh, Ms. Rumson."

Lara turned to her boss.

"Be in the library at nine."

"Yes, ma'am."

Miss Hawthorne lumbered down the hall, probably quite pleased.

Lara sighed. This wasn't an office. No wonder Miss Logan, the school's counselor, had a shit-eating grin on her face when Lara had met her. Logan probably occupied the former vice-principal's office.

"How are the children?"

Lara turned to see a woman with a broad smile.

"Excuse me?"

"How are the children?" she repeated, her voice a high-pitched screech.

"What children? School hasn't started yet."

"Oh, it's just an expression. I'm Miss Howard, the art teacher."

"Lara Rumson, vice-principal."

"Welcome to Vista Terrace. It's good to have you here."

"Thank you." Lara forced a smile. "I wish everyone shared your sentiment. This is my office. Or what they call an office."

Miss Howard's face drooped. "They put you in here?"

Lara nodded.

Miss Howard shook her head. "It's a shame. A crying shame." She smiled and disappeared down the hall.

Lara stepped into the room and her nostrils were filled with a clammy smell. She grimaced and began making a mental list. Bright light. Air freshener. Flowers. Lots of color. Sense of humor. The room was near the main office but cut off from the rest of the administration. Sitting in the chair, she half expected it to crumble into splinters. It didn't. She opened the desk drawers and found them empty. Lara rested her head on her hands for a moment, crestfallen by the disappointment of what had promised to be a step up in her career.

She wasn't certain how much time had passed.

"Ms. Rumson."

The voice came from above, emanating out of what must be part of an intercom system.

"Yes?" Lara spoke with trepidation.

"Miss Hawthorne needs to see you."

"Okay."

I've been summoned.

Lara pushed the rickety chair back and left her gloomy cell.

When Lara entered the office, the secretary marched over to Miss Hawthorne's open doorway. "Ms. Rumson is here."

The secretary turned to Lara and nodded.

Lara stepped into Miss Hawthorne's office. She was seated behind her desk, and Miss Logan, the counselor, sat in a chair next to her. The counselor had managed to wipe the shit-eating grin off of her face and appeared more sober. Miss Hawthorne gestured for Lara to sit, and she took a seat across from the principal.

"I'm listening." Miss Hawthorne gave Lara a hard look.

"Ma'am?"

"I'm listening to your concerns. Any concerns you have, bring them to me. I am here to listen to them. Do you have any concerns?"

Lara's peaches-and-cream complexion began to turn scarlet. "No, ma'am. None at present."

"If you have any concerns, you express them to me and only me. When you learn how things operate at Vista Terrace, you'll learn that I am the only person who can do anything about your concerns."

The counselor did not say a word. Then it suddenly clicked.

Miss Howard told Miss Hawthorne I complained about my office.

"You may go." Miss Hawthorne dismissed Lara with a wave of her hand. Lara got up from her chair and quickly left the room.

She moved through the main office without making eye contact with anyone and dug her hand into her purse as soon as she entered the hallway.

This is ridiculous. The art teacher is a rat.

She unscrewed the top on her aspirin bottle and, as soon as she turned the corner, ran smack into Kelvin Young. Her aspirin scattered all over the floor.

"I'm sorry! Are you okay?"

"Fine." Lara crouched down.

"Let me help you. I'll pick these up. Sorry about that."

"It's my fault. I wasn't watching where I was going."

Kelvin scooped up all the aspirin. "I guess the floor hasn't been cleaned."

"I'll throw them away." Lara held out her hand.

"No, I'll do it. No sense in both of us getting our hands dirty." Kelvin looked around. "You see a wastebasket?"

"There's one in my office."

About the only thing in the office.

Lara pointed to the room.

"That's your office?"

Lara nodded.

"I thought my classroom was bad." Kelvin tossed them into the trash can. "I was looking for you."

"What can I do for you?" Lara's temples were pounding.

His solid, muscular frame filled another polo shirt, this one a blazing bright green. His deep ebony skin contrasted strikingly with the color. Strong, muscular thighs pressed against the fabric of his khaki pants.

He's more handsome today than yesterday.

"There aren't any science textbooks in my room. Miss Hawthorne said they're in the book room and you have the key."

"I do." Lara grabbed the large ring from her desk. "Now all I have to do is remember which one is the book room. I got a tour a short while ago."

"Come on, we can find it."

Lara had to admit she liked his smile. Genuine, a quality sadly lacking in most men she'd dealt with in education. They always seemed so full of themselves. Kelvin came across as sincere.

But he was also a bit too good-looking. His playboy reputation preceded him, and she could see why. Women fawned over him. Many did presumably for his money, but all of them had to be swooning over his brawny body and movie star good looks.

They walked to the far end of the school. Lara recalled the book room was in one of the T-buildings, as they were called. The T stood for temporary because they were sort of like prefabricated rooms that could be removed if needed. Those rooms were much bigger than her so-called office.

Lara fiddled with the key ring. "Of course the keys aren't labeled."

"Can I help?"

"No, I've got to learn them anyway." She tried several keys before she found the right one.

The room was hot and dusty with a rancid odor. Lara found a switch and rows of dusty-covered lights flickered on.

"What do you need?"

Kelvin shrugged. "Seventh and eighth grade science. One of each to use to lesson plan until I get my roster."

Lara and Kelvin moved among the stacks. Some were labeled, some were not. Hard to believe this was a school in the service of educating children. The place was a disorganized mess.

"Be careful. Watch your step."

He was right. Junk plastered the floor. Fallen books, littered papers.

Unreal.

"Here's science. Oh, that's sixth grade." Lara peered at another shelf. "Can you see up there?"

Kelvin looked up. "Got it."

He pulled down a seventh and an eighth grade text.

"Do you need anything else while you're here?" Her voice wavered. She glanced around the cluttered, dirty shelves.

"I don't think so…unless there are any student workbooks to go with them."

"Let's look while we're here. Not sure I want to come back in here anytime soon."

"I'm sorry. I didn't mean to put you out."

"You're not. It's part of my job if I've got the key."

They moved deeper into the stacks.

"Not that I'm complaining," Lara added. "I'm here to do a job."

"So am I. Hey, was that really your office?"

Lara glared at him. "I'd rather not discuss it." She looked away. The magnitude of what she'd gotten herself into began to sink in. She'd left a cushy teaching job in a neighboring parish for this. Often, new gigs came with rocky starts, and she shouldn't let it get to her now. But it did.

"Did I say something wrong?"

Lara had her back to him. His strong, comforting hand squeezed her shoulder, and the tension melted. A wave of unfamiliar warmth slid through her body.

"I didn't mean to embarrass you. My classroom doesn't look any better."

His touch.

Lara relaxed, and she didn't want him to move his hand pressed against her shoulder. Of course, she couldn't stand there all day. They'd be missed. Lara turned to face Kelvin and placed her hand on his chest against one of his massive pectorals. It flexed, sending a shiver through her. She let out a slight gasp and her lips parted.

Kelvin moved closer, and his lips almost touched hers. His warm breath breezed against her. Her hand clenched against his chest, and her heart pounded even more urgently than her temples. The textbooks in his hand dropped to the floor.

She pushed away. "What time is it?"

He looked at his watch. "Five to nine."

"Shit! We need to be in the library at nine."

"You're right." Kelvin picked up the two textbooks he'd dropped. "I hope I didn't…"

"You didn't. Let's go. I have the impression Lady Hawthorne doesn't tolerate lateness."

Kelvin laughed.

Lara caught herself. "You didn't hear me say that."

They found their way out of the room and Lara locked the door. Her head spun. She couldn't believe she'd just allowed herself to be alone with a man. In fact, she couldn't remember the last time she had been in the same room with one.

**

"I'm going to drop these books off in my room."

Lara nodded. Kelvin hurried to his classroom and dropped off the texts. As he returned down the hallway toward the library, he passed an open door. Mr. Strode was seated at his desk, apparently in no rush to get to the nine o'clock meeting. Strode's room was a vast improvement over his own. The walls appeared to be freshly painted and the room's lighting bright. Strode looked up and back to his desk without acknowledging Kelvin.

If you're not in with the clique, you're out. I must be out.

Kelvin shook his head and made his way to the library. This was going to be a tough year, but he could handle it. And aside from his love of teaching, he could look forward to seeing Lara Rumson every day.

What just happened in the book room?

Lara was his superior and he'd almost kissed her. He wasn't supposed to do that, but he couldn't help it. Desire wasn't an emotion he could easily control. Fortunately, she hadn't made a big deal out of it.

When he reached the library, some of the staff chattered among themselves. Lara spoke with Miss Hawthorne. How hard had Hawthorne come down on her? Lara had been stressed out over something on the way to the book room.

"Maureen Howard."

Kelvin looked up. A woman extended her hand, and he shook it.

"I'm Kelvin Young. Science teacher and football coach."

"Happy to have you here! We need a good coach. Are you from the area?"

By now everyone likely knew he wasn't. "No, I was recruited from another district."

Miss Howard smiled and moved to another table.

Mr. Strode returned to his seat without so much as a nod to Kelvin. This was the first time Kelvin had become aware of the other man's height. He practically towered over Kelvin. He was also significantly older, probably in his mid to late forties.

"Any good places in Portsmith to hit a happy hour?"

This time Strode looked up. "I don't drink."

Strode seemed offended by Kelvin's gesture.

Another fun day.

Lara stood in front of the room, her hands clasped together. Kelvin wished he could do something to help her. Another staff member droned on and on about policies and procedures. By the time a break came, Kelvin was tired. He wanted to speak with Lara, but it appeared as though Hawthorne wasn't through with her.

Kelvin stopped by the office, and a woman seated behind a computer stared at him.

"No one's gonna clean that room out for you, Mr. Strode," she said.

An older woman appeared from a back office. "That's not Mr. Strode. That's the other one."

"Are you Mr. Young?" the first woman asked.

"Yes, ma'am."

"Are you from the Young family?"

"That's my last name," Kelvin answered, noncommittal. He hated that question.

"Are you married?"

Kelvin forced a smile. "Not at the moment. Have a nice day."

In the parking lot, Kelvin loitered until Lara came out of the building. She did not look happy.

"Would you like to go to lunch?"

Lara shook her head. "No, thank you. This is a working lunch for me. Miss Hawthorne's given me some tasks to complete."

Kelvin nodded. "You still need to eat. Come on. There's an Italian place I know of. The work can wait."

Lara met his gaze and, after a moment, nodded.

The Italian restaurant stood a good distance from Vista Terrace. Far enough that hopefully none of Kelvin's co-workers would spot him and ask why he was out to lunch with the vice-principal.

Shouldn't Lara be more worried about that? As an administrator, she had more to lose by the appearance of impropriety than he did. Damn, it was just lunch. They both needed to get over it.

But it was the atmosphere in the district. So much distrust. Resentment. Resistance against change.

Kelvin took a deep breath.

The smell of garlic filled his nostrils, and he hadn't even stepped out of the car yet. Freshly baked garlic bread. That was a good sign. Kelvin hadn't been to the restaurant before. In fact, he seldom ventured up to Portsmith to eat. But he had scoped it out on Google earlier today in anticipation of inviting Lara out to eat.

But why had he taken such an interest in her? He wasn't brown-nosing the boss. He couldn't care less about her status. They were in this together as a team.

And it wasn't purely sexual. He'd gone through his days of meeting a woman and getting her in bed after the first drink.

But he didn't think of Lara in those terms. He had no problem exuding confidence around a woman he wanted to nail. With Lara, he wasn't sure how to identify what was happening.

Intrigued. A bit off his game. And ready to find out more about her.

Lara had opened the passenger door before he'd had a chance to. She placed one shoe on the pavement, and he offered his hand. She accepted his help, and her velvety hand glided against his palm.

Kelvin's groin tightened when her flesh made contact with his. How could he be so vulnerable around her? If that was the right word. Not vulnerable. He hadn't met anyone like Lara before and didn't quite know how to handle her. Yet.

"Thank you." Her sunglasses enveloped her eyes and added to her aloofness.

Kelvin closed the car door and led her inside.

The place was dark and cozy and rather sparse for lunchtime. They were ushered to a quiet booth, and Lara removed her shades.

"Is this okay?" the hostess asked.

Lara nodded.

"Yes, thank you." Kelvin gestured for Lara to sit.

"It smells lovely." Lara gazed at the menu.

Even in the moody lighting of the restaurant, her emerald eyes glistened as she scanned the lunch specials.

A server placed two glasses of water on the red and white checkerboard tablecloth. "May I get you anything else to drink?"

"A Sprite," Lara said.

Not a Diet Coke this time.

"Water's fine."

"Do you need more time?"

Lara shook her head. "Cobb salad."

Kelvin glanced at the selections. "Fettuccine Alfredo."

The server took the menus and left them alone.

"I hope the service isn't slow here. I need to get back to work."

"It can wait. Everyone deserves a break."

Lara sighed. "You're right. We shouldn't be talking about work when we're off campus. How about a pact? We don't talk about work outside of work."

"Good deal." Kelvin had no problem coming up with topics. Her lips, plump as ballpark franks. Radiant eyes accented by long lashes. Two globes, pressed against the fabric of her blouse.

"You have quite a commute every morning, don't you?" He could listen to her silky voice all day.

"Bakersville. Forty-five minutes. It's not bad."

"My commute tops out at twenty. That's long enough for me."

"But you're new to the district, aren't you?"

"Yes. I worked in the neighboring district. Lester City. Still only twenty minutes away from my place."

Kelvin nodded. He couldn't believe he was on a lunch date with his vice-principal. But was it a date? They were just two colleagues going out to lunch. But were they colleagues? Lara outranked him.

"What's it like?" Lara asked.

"What?"

"Bakersville."

Kelvin shrugged. "Beautiful. It's been my home all my life. Quiet. Removed from the world in some ways. I like it. It's home. I guess I'd even call it tranquil."

Lara raised a brow. "Sounds too good to be true."

"Maybe I'll have to prove it to you." Kelvin smirked. Lara wouldn't step out of her comfort zone to venture out to Bakersville. Or would she?

"You've got nothing to prove to me, Mr. Young."

"Kelvin."

"Mr. Young."

"Even outside of work?"

"Yes." Lara's steely expression indicated she wasn't playing.

"Okay. We can't talk about work outside of work, yet we need to remain completely formal with one another at all times. Did I get that right?"

A corner of Lara's mouth turned up, transforming her from steely to wary.

Kelvin nodded. "Got it."

Maybe she does have a playful side.

The server placed a Sprite in front of Lara and moved on. Lara unwrapped the straw, placed it in her glass, and wrapped her luscious lips around the tip. The crimson shade of her lipstick stained the plastic tube.

"What's Bakersville like? Is it country?"

Kevin bristled at the word country. "No, I wouldn't say that. Not at all. At least, not in the sense that word is used in Louisiana. It's actually quite nice."

"I didn't mean to be unkind."

"It's a small town, but—"

"I know what you mean. Affluent."

Kelvin nodded.

"My family worked their way up to affluence." Lara frowned. "I'm sorry. There I go again. I'm not implying your family didn't. No offense."

"None taken."

"I'm just not clear-headed today. So much on my mind."

"What can I do to distract you?"

Lara played with the straw in her glass. "You already did by bringing me here. I appreciate that."

"It took some convincing. But it was well worth it." Kelvin met her gaze. Why did Lara intimidate him so? Something about her turned him from confident macho man into quivering schoolboy. Warmth rushed through his head.

"What part of town do you live in?"

"Highland Heights."

"I'm not familiar with it. Actually, I'm not familiar with

Portsmith much at all. I came up here often as a child with a family member, but not so much once I went off to college."

"Where did you go to school?"

"Morehouse."

Lara nodded. "I went to Louisiana State. Then Tech for my master's."

"I stopped after my bachelor's. Been teaching for eight years."

"Why Portsmith?"

"Dr. Hamilton is persuasive." Kelvin chuckled. "You just broke your own rule."

Lara smirked. "I wasn't speaking about Vista Terrace. I meant, if you work in Portsmith, won't you get a place here?"

"No. I'm fine with commuting."

"I don't know how you do it." Her full red lips wrapped around the straw again, and she sucked the liquid into her mouth.

Kelvin's cock throbbed in his pants. He had to stop this foolishness now. That wasn't why he'd asked Lara to lunch. More pressing matters were at hand. Such as, why did she hold such a powerful allure?

"I prefer my commute to be short." Lara blotted her lips.

"And sweet?"

Lara shot a glance at him that, for an instant, could cut through glass. Then she warmed. "Yes. Very sweet." Her gazed roamed for a moment. "With that long commute, when do you get your workout?"

35

"What do you mean?"

"To maintain your robust physique. You must spend hours in the gym."

She's checking out my body.

"I get up early."

"You've put a lot of work into staying in top shape."

Kelvin winced. Yeah, he had a good physique and had worked like hell to maintain it. But it hadn't always been that way. "I was a fat kid." His voice came out a whisper.

"Excuse me?"

"I was husky. Until I was around ten. Then my parents put me on a strict diet and exercise regime. I've had to work my butt off to maintain it ever since."

"Not just maintain it," Lara said. "You've built it."

"True. Bodybuilding is one of my passions."

Lara shook her head. "I can't picture you as a chubby kid."

"Oh, yeah. I was. Got my fair share of teasing."

"You mean bullying."

"No, we still called it teasing back then. I don't think it really qualified as bullying. Half the guys who teased me were tipping the scales. I guess they couldn't see the extra weight on themselves, just on me."

The images of those days flooded back to him. The taunting. The name-calling. His father refusing him desserts after dinner while everyone else ate theirs.

Yeah, I was a fat kid.

It hadn't been easy accepting the sacrifices and the hard work it had taken to lose the body fat and gain the muscle mass. When he'd started, his family's only concern was with him losing the body fat. Once he'd trimmed down, he'd become obsessed with building muscle.

"You've come a long way." Lara glanced away.

Kelvin nodded. "I have." He didn't necessarily agree with his own words.

What must she think of him now? A former fat kid revealing his past insecurities to his new vice-principal. Or perhaps his insecurities weren't in the past. At times, that little fat boy stared back at him from the mirror.

The fat boy who grew out of his clothing faster than his lanky younger brother. The trips to the store with his mother to buy the next size larger. The constant feeling of shame for a slow metabolism. Or for a love of southern cooking.

The server arrived and placed the plates of food before them. "Enjoy your lunch."

Kelvin stared down into his Fettuccine Alfredo with a sudden loss of appetite.

After they returned to the Vista Terrace parking lot, Kelvin dug into his pocket and pulled out a card. "Here's my number. Please call me if you need anything or if you just want to talk. I know it's gonna be rough for us."

Lara looked him in the eye. "I appreciate it." Lara placed the card in her purse and stepped out of his vehicle.

Kelvin wished he could do more. As an administrator, she probably absorbed more of the heat than a teacher. That frosty demeanor of hers was bound to crack at any time.

And he hoped they truly could make a difference at Vista Terrace. Dr. Hamilton expected that of them. The students did. The parents did as well. So much rode on the sweeping changes in the district. The school board had hired Hamilton for a reason, and Hamilton in turn aggressively recruited fresh blood for the district.

Only one obstacle stood in their way.

Miss Hawthorne.

After lunch, Hawthorne and her team gave marching orders for the rest of the afternoon. Procedures were stated, reviewed, and some even practiced. It came across as stuff that would be explained to first year teachers. In his former district, they never would have wasted time on this.

Before he left for the day, he hoped to chat with Lara. When he slipped by her office on his way out, Hawthorne was rattling off a list of things to do.

He got in his car and headed out of town.

Bakersville, located forty-five minutes south of Portsmith, had been Kelvin's home all his life. He'd purchased his own house not too far from his parents' estate. His home, modest by Young standards, fit his lifestyle. Quiet, comfortable, and—most important—all his.

He held a cold beer in one hand and a remote for the television in the other. With the sound muted, he could think while aimlessly flipping channels. Two science textbooks were sitting on his kitchen table, but he would get to that tomorrow. Tonight all he could think about was Lara Rumson.

He hadn't pursued any women lately. He usually had to politely rebuff them after they fawned all over him upon hearing his last name. Being a Young was a blessing and a curse.

The family resources had bought him a good education and could give him many opportunities in business if he chose to go that route, but also attracted the gold diggers in droves.

Lara seemed to have no interest in his name. In fact, she was barely interested in him. That was part of what made her so special. He could trust her since she didn't seem to have an agenda. Kelvin spent a lot of time alone because most women who approached him had some agenda based on the Young name.

I hope Lara's holding up okay.

Kelvin took a sip of beer, and the cold malt liquor coating his throat on a hot day. Hopefully, she would call if she needed anything. He sighed and looked up at the ceiling. What she needed was an assistant. It looked like Old Lady Hawthorne gave her more than her fair share of homework.

Should I look her up?

Kelvin decided against it. He didn't want to be intrusive. Starting next week, if she seemed overwhelmed, he would then take a more active approach.

This weekend's gonna drag.

Kelvin closed his eyes and longed for his tongue to mesh with hers. He wanted to hold her and press her close to him. How long would he have to wait to taste her? And why the hell was he thinking about her in that way? He hadn't accepted Hamilton's position in Portsmith just to chase tail. He'd done enough of that in his life.

A knock on the door forced his eyes open. He looked at the clock. It wasn't even six o'clock yet. He got up from the couch and opened the door.

"Hey! How ya doing?"

He blinked. He didn't recognize the woman. Oh, the hair. She had colored her hair a shade that was…unique.

"Fine."

"I lost my phone. That's why you haven't heard from me in so long."

But you obviously know where I live.

"Okay."

She made a slight move with her body that indicated she expected to come in. Kelvin did not move his arm off the doorway.

"So what's new?" she asked.

When did I meet her? Months ago?

"A lot actually. I just started a new job. I have a lot of work to do, in fact."

"On a Friday night?"

"Yes."

"Wow. What's gotten into you, playboy?"

Kelvin's facial muscles tensed, as he was unsure how to respond to that. He was aware of his reputation, but he didn't appreciate someone so blunt.

He chose his words carefully. "Nothing's gotten into me except that I'm in the middle of something."

The woman laughed. "Okay, I'll leave you alone to get back to—um—what you were doing."

Kelvin's icy stare hopefully gave her a hint.

"Catch up with you later!" She turned and walked away, and he shut the door. Why would a woman just show up after months without a word?

He returned to the living room to finish his beer. If anything, this was the time to put the bachelor life behind him. He had dated a lot, and it had gained him nothing but a bad reputation. He was thirty-one and deserved better than this.

Time to turn over a new leaf.

CHAPTER THREE

Lara craved a hot bath with Epsom salts, candles, and soft music. Her boss had given her an enormous amount of work to complete over the weekend. Some of the tasks were typically the responsibility of the counselor or the instructional coordinator. Hawthorne had dumped most of it on Lara.

She couldn't go to Dr. Hamilton. That would be going over Miss Hawthorne's head.

Never break the chain of command.

Besides, Dr. Hamilton had hired Lara to do a job, not to complain. He would expect her to deal with it, which was one of the reasons he had confidence in her. Hamilton had assessed the mess in this district and handpicked who he could trust to clean it up.

Developing a thicker skin might be a good idea. Hawthorne, controlling and demanding, knew what she wanted. Although that might be a good sign of leadership, she was not so good at delegating responsibility.

After pulling into her driveway, Lara dragged herself out

of the car. Inside, she kicked her shoes off and headed straight for the bathroom to get her soothing Epsom salt oasis started. Her phone rang and unfortunately the display indicated it was the school.

"Hello."

"Ms. Rumson, this is Miss Hawthorne. I forgot to mention one thing. Please email me each project as you complete it over the course of the weekend. Don't wait until Monday to turn it over to me all at once."

"Yes, ma'am."

"Have a lovely weekend."

Lovely.

Hawthorne hadn't said *nice* or *good.* She said *lovely.* Lara decided a nice glass of wine would be lovely with her bath. She turned on the hot water and, while the tub filled, went to the kitchen to pour some. A bottle of Chardonnay in the fridge was a welcome sight after the day she'd had.

Almost as good as the sight of Kelvin Young.

Strapping hunk. Good manners. Clearly well bred. Of course, he was from that Young family. They had more money than they knew what to do with. She liked Kelvin. He seemed grounded.

And he looks good.

He must've spent hours in the gym to get so robust. His muscles were well defined. Every cut and bulge evident, even when wearing his fine polo shirts.

Why am I thinking about him now?

The heat that had filled her body when he'd massaged her shoulder lingered in her mind. It was a heat she hadn't experienced before. A heat that radiated throughout her entire being. Lara hadn't made room for men as she relentlessly pursued her career and furthered her education. Now, Kelvin had walked right into her life.

What next?

Probably nothing. He was a teacher, and she was an administrator who outranked him. It shouldn't go any further.

Enough about Kelvin. She shouldn't be thinking about men now, not with all the tension at Vista Terrace. First years were always challenging. This was her first year as an administrator. She might as well get used to it.

Or vent to someone outside of the school system. Like Cassie. A close friend, Cassie could be counted on for being a good listener. But Lara didn't feel like burdening anyone with venting this weekend. If she called Cassie at all, it would be to catch up or go out and have some fun.

Lara placed the bottle back in the fridge and went to check on her bath. She sprinkled some Epsom salt evenly throughout the tub. Epsom salt was always evident in her grandmother's house, which was just one of many things Lara had learned from her. It soothed sore feet or a sore body after a rough day.

Satisfied the water was ready, she placed a few candles around the edge of tub and lit them. She skipped turning on any music. Her head was getting that aching feeling just thinking about the mountain of work she had to do for her boss. She sniffed the light fragrance of her wine and took a sip.

Lara slid her body into the wonderful heat of the bath.

Nice and hot. She could smell the salts over the scent of her candles. The water soothed and comforted her body. Nothing like a good bath. No, it was better than good. It was lovely.

**

Lara dreaded the sound of her alarm clock like she dreaded a downpour without an umbrella. It had been a restless night with barely any sleep. She was overtired—that was the problem. Hawthorne had run her ragged all weekend. Revise this, fix that, redo this schedule, trash that one and start over. Lara crawled over the edge of her bed. It was 4:40 a.m. The alarm would be going off in twenty minutes, and it wasn't worth shutting her eyes for such a short time. She rolled out of bed and got the coffee started.

Today was Monday. The children started school on Tuesday, which gave Hawthorne another full day to terrorize her. Lara hoped once classes were in session she would have some leeway to actually do her assigned job.

She glanced at the table where his card sat.

Kelvin Young.

She had gazed at the card several times over the weekend and imagined those massive arms wrapped around her. Strong. Protective. Satisfying. Filling her with a comfort she hadn't known with men.

Could he?

For Lara, the focus of the past several years had been career, career, and repressed sexuality.

And here I am.

She poured a cup of coffee. She usually took cream, but today she was drinking it black. She needed all the strength she could muster to face this day.

Lara pulled into Vista Terrace shortly after seven o'clock. The light was on in Miss Hawthorne's office. Did she drag the head custodian out of bed each morning to open up the school?

"This will be the first day the full staff is here. I will introduce them to you. We're meeting at eight in the library." Miss Hawthorne handed her a thick packet of paper. "This is our school's disciplinary plan. I'd like you to look it over and offer any suggestions."

"Yes, ma'am." Lara figured as long as she kept saying *yes, ma'am* she could make it through the day.

"Did you pick up what I asked you for?"

"Yes, ma'am."

"You're here early. That shows commitment on your part." Hawthorne nodded. "You may go."

Lara headed for the library. Her office was far too dingy and depressing. She suspected she'd be spending as little time as possible in there.

When she reached the library, she wasn't surprised to find it locked. She marched up and down the breezeway until she found Lewis.

"Good morning, Mr. Lewis. Will you open the library for me?"

"Good morning, Mizz Rumson. Can't open anything without Mizz Hawthorne's permission."

"Can you ask her permission?"

Mr. Lewis pulled a two-way radio from his hip. "Mizz Hawthorne."

"Yes," crackled the voice through the well-worn radio.

"Can I open the library for Mizz Rumson?"

"Yes, please do."

Lara smirked. Hawthorne had nothing but rules.

"How are you doing today, Mr. Lewis?"

"Just fine, ma'am."

"Are you always here so early?"

Lewis nodded. "Gotta open the school up at six. Earlier if Mizz Hawthorne calls me."

Lara could only imagine how many times Hawthorne called him early. Lewis was a pleasant-looking man, probably in his forties. When she had shaken his hand, her first day on campus, it was rough and calloused. He had the hands of a laborer.

Lewis unlocked the door and held it open for Lara.

"Thank you, Mr. Lewis."

"No problem, Mizz Rumson. You have a good day. Don't work too hard." Lewis reached for his radio and clicked it off. Then he lowered his voice. "She'll work you to death if you let her."

Lara's expression froze. She wasn't certain how to take his comment. Lewis must be a very observant man. Then again, school custodians had the run of building.

A large supply closet stood in the rear of the library. Lara found some plastic tablecloths and spread them out over the tables. There were also quite a few cheap centerpiece items that looked like they'd come from a dollar store. Actually, the supply closet was loaded with stuff. Large coffee urns, serving trays, utensils. Someone kept it well stocked.

Lara placed the centerpieces on the tables. Her body's temperature spiked as high as an elevator ride at the Space Needle. Kelvin stood in the doorway.

He was smartly dressed in chinos that were too tight for him, and another brightly colored polo wrapped around his muscular body. As always, he dressed to show off his perfectly sculpted physique.

The tingling in her lady bits signaled danger. No one else had arrived, and she found herself alone with Kelvin. Heat surged through her.

"Good morning." He flashed a smile.

"What are you doing here so early?" She avoided his gaze, hoping he wouldn't notice her unease. Her lack of experience with men was embarrassing.

"I have a habit of getting to work early. May I sit here?"

Lara smirked. "I don't think we have assigned seats." Of course she wanted him to sit near her. What woman wouldn't?

His robust frame filled the chair next to her. She caught a subtle whiff of his woody cologne.

"How was your weekend?" Kelvin's velvety voice commanded her complete attention.

"Lovely. Yours?"

"Busy. Lesson planning."

"Surely you didn't spend the whole weekend lesson planning?"

Kelvin shook his head. "No, but I did want to get a head start. I like to be prepared." He gestured to the paperwork she'd put on the table. "What are you reading?"

"Nothing interesting." Lara couldn't concentrate on that now anyway. She was too tired from a lack of sleep.

But his good looks are better than caffeine.

His face relaxed, he sat with his shoulders straight, chest thrust out, and his big hand dwarfed his coffee cup.

"I guess we get to meet the rest of the staff today," Kelvin said.

"Yeah, the support staff."

Lara met his eyes in a moment of silence. So warm. Could he be as genuine as he appeared? Her nipples swelled against her bra. She had to look away and focus on something else if she was going to function at her job.

"Need some help?" Kelvin asked.

"Yes." Lara tossed him the keys to her car. "The donuts are in the back seat. It's the white Camry."

"Got it."

Lara gathered some napkins, Styrofoam cups, coffee stirrers, nondairy creamer, and other assorted stuff. She arranged all of that on display in front of the library.

Kelvin returned with the boxes of donuts stacked on his muscular forearms.

"Where do you want them?"

Lara pointed to a table. "Right there is fine."

"What's next?" His robust arms glistened.

"I'll need some help with the coffee urns. They're back here."

Lara led the way to the supply room.

How does he always look so good?

Even at the crack of dawn, Kelvin looked well rested. She was grateful she walked ahead of him, otherwise she'd have to ogle his buns.

Although with a body that good, Kelvin would look great in anything.

The cramped supply closet didn't offer much elbowroom.

"Thank you," Kelvin said.

"What are you thanking me for? I should be thanking you."

"Thank you for allowing me to help you." There wasn't a hint of insincerity in his voice.

"Are you always such an angel?"

Kelvin shook his head. "No. Most definitely not…" He laughed. "I know you've been overworked and I want to help if I can."

"You're very kind."

Lara placed her hand on his forearm. A rush of electricity surged through her body just by touching his skin. The short-sleeved shirt he wore revealed his smooth arms. He moved close and placed his arms around her, and he leaned in to kiss her. An even stronger heat raged through her body. His lips found hers. Lara squeezed his hard, muscules and closed her eyes.

This is crazy.

Her legs went weak, about to give out. The heat in her core surged, and her body shivered with a need she'd fought all her life. In Kelvin's arms, her body went limp and her pulse raced.

She had work to do and the staff would be arriving soon.

But his touch aroused her and his fresh taste made her want more, even though they only had a moment together. Lara gripped Kelvin's arm and squeezed it.

"Kelvin, I can't do this. I have to finish preparing—"

"I know," Kelvin said.

Lara released her grip and slipped out of his arms.

"Kelvin—Mr. Young, will you grab the coffee urn?" Lara snatched a large tin of coffee, opened the door, and quickly left the room.

What the hell am I doing?

Lara dropped the coffee on the table, then headed for the ladies' room. Her knees shook and hands trembled. After she unlocked the door to the adult restroom, she glanced around quickly. She was alone.

Her heart palpitated, and she held her palm to her chest.

How many times can I run to the restroom when I'm upset?

Clutching her handbag, she tried to fight conflicting emotions. She ducked into a stall just in case someone came in. Men weren't a part of her life. She wanted nothing to do with them, except a few furtive glances here and there. She couldn't be with a man. Not after—

But Kelvin Young wasn't just any man. Something about him made her lady bits prickle in a way that was foreign to her. She responded to him and there had to be a reason.

How can I be so stupid?

A new job. A new district. A new position. First-time administrator. Why mess it up over a guy? She'd never allowed a man to affect her this way and she wasn't about to start now.

After she took several deep breaths, she left the stall and checked her appearance. She wiped off the smudges and reapplied her lipstick. Her heart pounded. That wasn't just a kiss, although Lara couldn't find the right words to describe it. From the heat that radiated through her body, he had to be the most sensual man she'd ever met.

And dangerous.

After what had happened to her in her adolescence, she didn't want to be near a man. Luke had ruined her. Yet despite the trauma haunting her, desire took her by surprise.

Kelvin's allure was no match for her will.

Back in the library, Kelvin had gotten the coffee going for her. Unfortunately, he was still the only staff member who'd arrived. She didn't relish being in the room alone with him. No fault of his, of course. It was entirely her self-inflicted discomfort.

"I'm looking forward to classes beginning tomorrow."

Lara averted her gaze and pretended to smooth out a tablecloth. "I am as well. The staff has too much time on their hands without the children here."

"How so?"

"Forget I said that, Mr. Young."

"You can call me Kelvin."

Lara faced him. "No, I shall not. And you will address me as Ms. Rumson. I hate it when staff uses first names while at school. It always slips out in front of the children and that's unprofessional."

"Understood…Ms. Rumson." He winked, and Lara caught a glimpse of jest in his gaze.

She turned her attention to the dreary disciplinary plan she was supposed to be reading. This wasn't the time for charm. She stole another glance at Kelvin. His forearms were almost as huge as his biceps.

She grabbed her paperwork and contemplated leaving when that snake Maureen Howard slithered into the room. In a way, Lara was glad she'd learned Miss Howard was a spy on day one. That saved Lara the trouble of ever speaking to that fink again.

Stop it. Now.

Adopting a positive and welcoming attitude were good qualities for a new administrator. She had to start behaving like one.

**

Kelvin's gaze didn't stray from Lara. She appeared stressed.

She had a busy weekend.

Lara put on a professional front that all had gone well when it most likely hadn't. Still, her beauty hadn't faltered. Her golden hair framed her face, and those shimmering blue eyes captivated him.

One of Hawthorne's cronies appeared and passed out an agenda. Kelvin was grateful to see there was time allotted in the afternoon for teachers to work on their classrooms. His was a mess and needed a lot of work. Why had Hawthorne let the previous teacher leave it in such a deplorable condition? Kelvin would never have done that.

He and the other *new folk*, as Hawthorne referred to them, were introduced to the rest of the staff. Then, Hawthorne and her administrative team led the teachers through yet another professional development activity, and Kelvin could hear his stomach gurgling. He was relieved when Hawthorne finally dismissed them at 10:45.

Kelvin milled about outside the library until Lara emerged.

"That was a good presentation. Can I get you some lunch?"

"I have to work through lunch," Lara said.

"You need to eat something. I'll pick something up for you."

"Don't trouble yourself."

"It's no trouble. I'm starving so I've got to eat something. Sandwiches okay?"

"Mr. Young, I'm fine, and I have work to do." Lara hurried away.

This is gonna be a challenge.

He followed Lara to her poor excuse for an office.

"Am I disturbing your work?"

"Do you need something, Mr. Young?"

"Why don't you eat something?"

"I will."

"I'm gonna run to the deli and pick up sandwiches. What can I get you?"

Lara flashed an icy gaze at him, then immediately thawed. "Tuna fish. On toast."

"Got it."

"No, I got this one." Lara reached for her purse.

"Don't worry about it." Kelvin didn't give her a chance to reach for any money.

He ordered a provolone and smoked turkey for himself and returned to Lara's office at Vista Terrace.

Lara looked up at him but said nothing. She was beautiful even when she glared, but there had to be a lot going on in her head that she hadn't communicated.

"Do you think we're the only two at this school hired by Dr. Hamilton?" Kelvin asked.

Lara nodded. "It's obvious from Miss Hawthorne's introductions."

Kelvin laughed. "You're right. She fawned all over Mr. Strode and the others and glossed over us. What do you know about Strode?"

"Nothing except that he transferred from another school within the district."

"He gives me the cold shoulder." Distant and secretive were the first two words that came to mind. Strode seemed cut off from the rest of the faculty. He came across as someone who wanted nothing to do with anybody.

"I wouldn't worry about it. Teachers can be petty. Do the best job you can do for your students and for the boys you'll be coaching."

"I'm gonna stay focused on that. Listen, after lunch, I'm gonna work on my classroom. If you have time, and I don't want to take you away from what you're doing, will you have a look? I mean, before Hawthorne sweeps through."

Lara stared at him for a moment. "You've taught before. You know what you're doing."

"Yes, but a second pair of eyes would help."

Lara shrugged. "Okay."

She touched his hand, and Kelvin took her hand in his. Something brushed against his palm. "Lunch is on me."

Kelvin opened his hand and spotted cash. "Don't be silly."

"I insist." Lara's tone indicated there'd be no arguing.

After lunch, Kelvin tackled cleaning his classroom. The desks all had to be wiped down with a strong disinfectant cleaner. There were piles of papers and junk that seemed to have been abandoned by the previous occupant. Kelvin needed to clear all of that out of the way for his own stuff. Posters and signs were half torn off the walls, as though someone had made a hasty and sloppy attempt at removing them.

Room 114 down corridor C was going to be Kelvin's new home. He had better make the most of it. Curiously, Mr. Strode's room was also on corridor C, and his room was virtually spotless.

Miss Hawthorne appeared in the doorway just as Kelvin put some serious elbow grease into cleaning the desks.

"Mr. Young, beginning at two o'clock, I'll be doing a walk-through to inspect the rooms."

"Yes, ma'am."

"You have quite a bit of work to do. Those walls have to have something on them, you know."

"Yes, I'll take care of it. I'm committed to being the best I can be for my students."

Miss Hawthorne's gaze wandered around the room before coming back to him. "You come from a small school in a small school district. This is a big school with big challenges."

"I'm up to them, ma'am."

"We'll see."

Kelvin took a deep breath. His focus was on educating and coaching children. He was not about to let Miss Hawthorne's feelings about him or how he had been hired get in the way. She could direct all that negativity at Dr. Hamilton, but of course she wouldn't since he was now her boss.

He worked up a sweat, and eventually the room looked better than before. He hung posters and charts on the walls, arranged the desks neatly, and cleared away a lot of clutter on the countertops.

"Not bad." Lara stood in the doorway gazing around the room. With her back straight, her breasts thrust forward.

Kelvin's voice came out barely above a whisper. "Thank you. All it took was a little effort."

"I might have you do your magic on my office."

His face brightened. "I can help you with that."

"Just kidding, I can manage on my own. I admire your decorating skill."

"One of many." His cock swelled against his thigh. Why did he allow himself to be distracted by her?

Lara stepped into the room, her chin high and her hips swaying. "I would say you're prepared for Miss Hawthorne's walk-through."

"She did a walk-through earlier to remind me of the walk-through. She was somewhat…condescending."

Lara looked at him. "Mr. Young, be careful what you say and to whom you say it. You don't have to worry about me, but everyone else is suspect. I've already learned that the hard way."

"Really? What happened?"

"Nothing I wish to repeat right now."

Her vulnerability, even in her tough position, struck him as attractive. He needed to be there for her.

Kelvin stepped closer to her. "Do you think my room will pass the Hawthorne inspection?"

"Who knows?" She looked away from him. "Where did you get the posters? I like them."

"I had most of them in my car."

Kelvin moved closer to her. He wanted to take Lara into his arms and hold her firmly against his chest. Her hand squeezed his arm. More specifically, she squeezed his bicep.

"I need to get back to work."

Her touch feels so good.

A rush of adrenaline had shot through him when her hand touched him. Perhaps it had been a rush of testosterone, because her touch made his temperature rise. He wanted her in a way he hadn't wanted a woman in a long time.

The question is when.

CHAPTER FOUR

Lara hurried briskly down the corridor.

I touched it.

She quickly removed her compact from her bag to check if her face was flushed. Fortunately, it wasn't.

I touched his bicep.

It was the largest bicep she had ever seen on a man. He was all muscle and could be a competitive bodybuilder with a bit more work.

It's rock hard.

The waves of warmth that ran through her were too much to handle. She'd had to get out of that classroom. The force that had shuddered through her when her hand touched that massive muscle made her light-headed. The corridor wasn't air conditioned, and hopefully she wouldn't faint before she made it back to her office.

Kelvin Young entranced her. No man should be that gorgeous. He had that perfect dark cocoa complexion, which he accented with those brightly colored shirts. He was thoughtful and well mannered, which placed him above ninety-five percent of the men out there. And he was a certifiable hunk.

I didn't want to let go.

But it wasn't merely physical. Something else had happened, and she couldn't quite put it into words. What she experienced when with Kelvin went beyond his obvious physical attributes. She trusted him. Enjoyed his company. Heck, he'd even lured her away from her job duties to a relaxing lunch.

No man had done that. At least, not one she'd trusted.

She had to work with him, so she needed to get a grip on herself—and not him. She wasn't sure how much contact she would have with the teachers. It looked as though Miss Hawthorne was giving her a little bit of everything. Actually, Hawthorne was giving her a lot of everything.

Lara returned to her office but didn't get much work done. Her boss summoned her to go over the schedule for tomorrow. The first day of school for the students had arrived.

Great.

She should have a tee shirt made that said, *Vice-principals do it all*, but that would probably not go over well with Miss Hawthorne. Lara wasn't afraid of hard work. She had no problem rolling up her sleeves and doing what needed to be done, but there had to be a limit. And it was up to her to set those limits.

But she'd gone through her master's in educational leadership to get out of the classroom and serve children in a different manner. This morning, she'd served coffee and donuts.

Within a short time, she was called to Miss Hawthorne's office again, and the principal briefed Lara on what to look for during the walk-through. Hawthorne wanted to see clean rooms, neatly arranged desks, and wall displays that promoted literacy.

She walked down the corridors by Miss Hawthorne's side and inspected each room. Hawthorne gave specific comments of praise, pointing out such things as the placement of the materials, specific arrangements of desks, and choice of display posters. She seemed particularly pleased with Mr. Strode's room—going on and on about how literacy-rich his walls were, how he'd put so much hard work into his room, and anything else she could think of.

When Hawthorne reached Mr. Young's room, she gazed around for a long time.

"Colorful bulletin boards," Miss Hawthorne finally said and left the room.

Lara met Kelvin's gaze for a moment. He had clearly put a lot of effort into his room. He smiled at her, but there was nothing he could do to please someone like Hawthorne.

After the walk-through was done, Hawthorne rattled off more tasks for Lara to complete. She sat down at her desk, overwhelmed with an unsettled feeling in her stomach, and she questioned if she could handle this job. The pressure pounded in her head again, but she shook it off. She was not about to become dependent on pain relievers.

"How's it going?"

Kelvin stood in her doorway looking gorgeous. She didn't usually choose that word to describe a man, but in

Kelvin's case, it certainly fit. She breathed easier at the sight of him. Her body relaxed, and the stress of the job faded away.

"I'm fine," Lara lied.

"Did I pass inspection?"

"I would say so. I'm sure Miss Hawthorne would have said something if not."

"Can I help you with anything?"

"No, nothing right now, thank you." Lara found it a struggle to take her eyes off of him. His broad smile melted her stoic front, and his presence turned up the heat.

And there he was, offering to help her again when it was actually her job to help and support him. Kelvin was a gem. His sincerity was what attracted her to him. Not just his brawn.

"If there's anything I can do for you, please let me know."

"Mr. Young, I am here to help you."

Kelvin stepped farther into her office. He smoldered with sensuality. There was a look in his eyes that she recognized, although it was not a look she had ever welcomed from a man. She wanted Kelvin but had enough sense to know this wasn't the place. Her lady parts had missed the memo on that one. Her nipples pebbled, and her core tingled.

"I really need to finish up my work."

Kelvin nodded. "I was hoping you could take a break."

"Not now."

"I'm done here for now. You still have my card?"

"Yes."

"Call me if you need anything. And I'll see you at open

house tonight." Kelvin gave her a wink and left her office. Her eyes dropped down to those round buns outlined so perfectly through his trousers.

How am I supposed to concentrate?

Lara reviewed her laundry list of instructions regarding preparations for open house. She'd do what she could, then slip home to change.

Lara got busy with the agenda, but Kelvin was still on her mind. She liked his attention. He wasn't pushy. But she wanted to make certain there wasn't any conflict of interest. It might not look good to the staff if she was seen with him. Some could interpret the time they spent speaking with one another as favoritism.

Perhaps she read too much into it.

If she planned to survive at Vista Terrace and make a name for herself, she needed to retain some of her individuality. She couldn't be a yes-man to Miss Hawthorne all the time, although it certainly seemed to be keeping the peace for now. That wouldn't last all year, nor would she expect Hawthorne to be satisfied by that simple response for much longer. There would always be challenges ahead. By being herself, Lara could face them and move forward.

Lara asked Lewis to help her set up some tables for open house where the students could pick up their schedules. She made signs indicating where to line up by the first letter of the student's last name, put up signs pointing to the various corridors, and wrote an agenda for Miss Hawthorne to approve. The afternoon flew by just as Lara hoped it would.

"I'm heading home to change. I won't be long."

Miss Hawthorne raised an eyebrow. "Are you satisfied everything's in order?"

"Yes, ma'am." Lara forced her best smile.

"You may go."

I wasn't asking for permission.

Lara didn't need much time, so she got in her car and enjoyed a leisurely ride home. Rather than turn on the air conditioner, she rolled the windows down and enjoyed the afternoon warmth.

At home, she got out of her clothes and took a quick shower. Tired of the corporate look, she chose something more casual. A nice dress and not-so-sensible shoes. The vibrant red and white cotton fabric was a far cry from her tailored suits. It suited her well. As she checked out her outfit in the mirror. Would it turn Kelvin's head?

Why am I thinking about him?

Because he was kind. Generous with his time and attention. He made a sincere effort to get to know her. Despite the physical moment between them, he'd made no blatant overtures. A gentleman.

She'd never dressed for a man in her life, and she sure as hell was not going to start now. That little ache between her legs frightened her. Why now?

**

An hour or so later, Lara stood in the auditorium and listened to Miss Hawthorne pontificate on how Vista Terrace was *the best* and offered *the best* education for middle school students in the parish. Lara admired school pride and was all for it, but the principal did have a tendency to go on and on.

Miss Hawthorne passed the mic to Lara. "My name is Lara Rumson. I am the new vice-principal at Vista Terrace. I am new to this school and this school district, but most of all, I'm here to ensure your boys and girls have a successful year."

Lara almost finished there but quickly added, "I am honored to work under the leadership of Miss Hawthorne." Lara handed the mic to Miss Logan. One thing Lara had learned about Hawthorne was that she loved to have her ego stroked. Since Lara was already a target, she might as well ease the blows whenever possible.

Kelvin, from the back of the room, winked at her.

Miss Hawthorne dismissed the teachers to their classrooms ahead of the parents so they could be at the door ready to greet them. Lara wanted to give Kelvin thumbs up for good luck, but he was already out the door.

Miss Logan had been eyeing her. It might have been Lara's imagination, but Logan seemed to have been watching Kelvin as well.

Did she notice us exchange glances?

Lara's responsibilities were not all that demanding for open house. She passed out brochures, answered questions from parents, grandparents and other relatives, and directed traffic. She could have used a map, as she wasn't all that familiar with the school herself. Several times she had to depend on Sonny, the nighttime custodian, to help her tell parents where to go.

She strolled back into the auditorium. Fortunately, she

wasn't in charge of refreshments. The coordinator and the art teacher were doling out punch and cookies to eager parents. Some of them appeared to have brought not only their middle school children but also their kids of all ages.

Finally, an announcement came over the intercom to wrap it up. Lara did her part straightening out chairs in the auditorium. She made herself busy rather than wait for Miss Hawthorne to give orders.

The families filed out, and Miss Hawthorne stood by the exit and thanked them for coming. She didn't move from the door until every parent had left.

"Run a sweep of the school. Make certain none of the parents or children remain in the building."

"Yes, ma'am."

Lara walked up and down each corridor. Some teachers were still tidying up their rooms, but Lara noted that most of them had left. Sonny began sweeping the auditorium.

"All families are gone, Miss Hawthorne. Just a few teachers left."

"Stay until the last one leaves, then make sure Sonny knows you're going."

"Yes, ma'am."

Lara stood by the door as Hawthorne left the building. After a long exhale, Lara headed back down the corridors.

Several teachers passed her on the way out. In fact, the only one who remained by the time she finished was Kelvin. Lara leaned against the doorframe and watched him. He appeared to be lost in some kind of work.

His focus and devotion, two more of his admirable

qualities, impressed her. Kelvin had been in the profession for eight years yet still worked tirelessly.

"What are you doing?"

"Just working."

Of course working. What else?

"Everyone's left."

Everyone except me.

Kelvin smiled. "I'm not everyone. Can you close the door? It keeps the room cool."

I'm the one who needs to keep cool.

The corridors were not air conditioned, and teachers were encouraged to keep their doors closed. As Kelvin jotted down notes, the muscles in his forearm flexed with each stroke of his pen.

Kelvin looked up from his work. "How did it go tonight?"

"Not bad. Good turnout."

Kelvin nodded. "I met a few parents and my future football stars."

I bet he's a good coach.

So loyal and dedicated to his work. Based on what she'd gleaned about his character so far, Lara suspected he coached for the love of the game and not because it was just part of the job. He made a good role model. In some distant way, he reminded her of her brother, Luke. He had been passionate about football as well and would sit for hours on the couch watching games. But Luke was no role model. He had, temporarily, turned Lara's world into a nightmare.

Can I move past that? Can I finally let go with a man and not be burdened by that nightmare?

Kelvin packed up his things.

"I didn't mean to rush you."

"You didn't. I've spent enough time at Vista Terrace today." Kelvin headed toward her. Although Lara stood with her back to the door, she didn't move. Her gaze locked on his. The ache between her legs hadn't subsided. It only increased and surged whenever he came near her.

Years of longing and repression melted away at the sight of him. That had to mean something. Could the denial be coming to an end? Could she finally reclaim her sexuality after what Luke had done to her so long ago? If anyone could make that happen, it had to be Kelvin Young.

He placed his briefcase on the floor. "Everyone's gone?"

Lara nodded.

"We're alone."

"Yeah," Lara croaked.

"I like being alone with you."

"Kelvin…" She reached out and absently rested her hand on his forearm. That muscular forearm she'd just watched flex as he worked.

His arms snaked around her. One pressed against her back and the other touched her butt. Kelvin moved his lips to hers and kissed her, mouth open, tongue meeting hers. Lara moaned, fire raging through her. His kisses made her sex ache.

Waves of warmth rumbled up and down her body as his wet kisses became more intense. She threw her arms around his neck and held his head in place. She didn't want him pulling away.

But he did.

Kelvin's lips moved down to her throat, and Lara let out a gasp. He found one of her soft zones and it made her moist. She shivered as his tongue rolled up and down her flesh and his hands moved from her butt up to her breasts. Fire raged through her when he gripped her breasts with his big hands and played with her nipples. They swelled at his touch, and he put his face between her soft globes. He let out a low growl as his tongue flicked against her flesh.

"Kelvin," she whispered.

His hand caressed her mound and rubbed her sweet spot. Lara's legs went weak. "Kelvin." When she said his name again, it wasn't a whisper. She became wet, her body trembled, and her breathing increased. He dropped to his knees and pulled at her soaked panties. He slipped his head under her dress and his tongue probed her velvety folds.

"Kelvin!" she cried. She was close to exploding. She grabbed the back of his head because she needed something to grip. With her other hand, she braced herself against the doorframe, otherwise her knees wouldn't hold her up. His tongue probed her deeper and his thumb twirled over her spot. Her body was on fire and she couldn't hold back. She shuddered and let out a cry from deep inside her gut as she exploded in a blinding, psychedelic orgasm. He held her body tightly as she shook and twitched.

Lara took a few deep breaths as her legs still quivered. He hadn't moved his head, and his tongue continued to explore her. With a flushed face, she tried to regulate her breaths.

Her back stood against the door and his hands had a firm

grip. She tried to slip away, but his tongue still danced inside of her. She pushed against his head but he didn't move.

"Kelvin." The name barely came out through her deep breaths.

She dropped her hand down to his shoulder and squeezed his hard muscle. His tongue did not move from her folds.

"Kelvin, I need to go."

Kelvin mumbled something, but she couldn't hear what he said. She was still light-headed from the torrential orgasm. Then it registered in her mind. Kelvin had said, *"No, you need to come."*

His mouth sucked on her nub and his fingers roamed inside her channel. Lara shook her head but to no avail. The wave rumbled through her whole being, and her knees gave away. Kelvin held her body up with his strong arms. He hoisted her up where her feet were no longer touching the ground. She cried out a loud, guttural moan that probably reverberated down the hallways.

Lara's legs were on Kelvin's shoulders, and he was on his knees holding her up.

We must look ridiculous.

"Let me down."

Kelvin gingerly guided Lara's feet back to the ground. She looked away for a moment, trying to collect herself. When she peered at Kelvin, his face glistened. He breathed heavily as well.

Amazing he didn't suffocate.

Lara pulled her panties up and straightened her dress. She was afraid to look in a mirror. The only thing she wanted to do was get out of there.

Kelvin stood up. "Would you like to—"

"No." Lara turned and opened the door. She stepped into the hallway and froze. Sonny stood right outside, mopping the floor.

CHAPTER FIVE

He had his back to her but that didn't mean anything. With all the sounds that had emanated from her, Sonny had to have heard everything. Humiliation swept through her and she couldn't move. She froze from the horror of what that meant. Sonny knew.

"I'll walk you to your car." Kelvin touched her arm.

She pulled away and didn't face him. "No. Miss Hawthorne gave me strict orders to clear the building. Go."

"That's okay, I think we're the last ones."

"Good night, Mr. Young." Her voice could cut glass.

Kelvin hesitated for a moment before making his way down the corridor. His footsteps echoed in the deafening silence.

Numb, Lara returned to the classroom and sat—her hopes, dreams, and aspirations now shattered. Sonny had heard what went on in this classroom, and it would be all over the school tomorrow. It didn't have to go any further than Miss Hawthorne's ears, and she'd be fired.

Won't I?

What she'd done tonight was wrong. Vice-principals

couldn't fraternize with the teachers, in or out of school. How would that look? Accusations of favoritism and who knows what else could be hurled at her if she stayed.

Perhaps I'll resign.

The best thing to do would be to go to Hamilton, thank him for his trust in her, and apologize for betraying it.

That's selfish.

She couldn't think just of herself. Kelvin's job was at stake as well.

Hawthorne would probably call them into her office, give them a chance to explain, and then offer them the opportunity to resign. Or dismiss them on the spot.

She wouldn't put anything past Hawthorne. It would probably delight her to no end to be handed a reason to ditch Hamilton's picks.

Her body shook at facing her boss over something as stupid as an indiscretion. Over something she'd done in a classroom with a man that she hadn't even done in private.

"Anything I can do for you, Miss?"

Lara's head snapped up, her face flushed crimson.

Sonny loomed in the doorway.

Lara shook her head.

"You look a bit distressed, Miss. Anything wrong?"

Lara's eyes welled. Plenty was wrong. Her sexuality, purposely repressed for so long, had come roaring out with a vengeance tonight. That was wrong. The timing was wrong. The place was wrong. And—

"This is the last wing I'm mopping tonight and I'm outta here."

Lara tried to keep her voice steady. "Oh, you leave that early?"

"Yes, Miss. Night custodians are on a half shift. Fo' hours and we out."

How could she face anyone at Vista Terrace tomorrow?

"You sho' I can't do anything for you, Miss?"

"No, Sonny. I don't think there's anything anyone can do for me at this point."

"What's troubling you tonight?"

"My own stupidity."

Sonny pulled up a chair. "If you don't mind me saying so, Miss, that Mr. Young is a nice guy, so far as I can tell. I just met him the other day. But I known of him befo' he come here."

"He's a notorious playboy, and I was foolish enough to—"

"Now, Miss. Don't you be getting yourself all embarrassed over nothing."

"But that's not like me. I don't do things like that. Ever."

"So, what does that tell you?"

Lara met his gaze. "What do you mean?"

"If you don't do things like that, ever, but you did tonight, doesn't that tell you that maybe it's time you do?"

Lara didn't quite follow his logic. "Sonny, I made a mistake that could cost me my career."

Sonny shook his head. "Public education is full of folks who make mistakes. Some every day and they keeps their jobs."

She lowered her gaze. "Not what I did."

His loud, boisterous laugh startled her. "That and more.

Miss, this ain't no wherever you came from. This is Vista Terrace. And it's not just here; it's all over Portsmouth ISD. Don't know where you came from, but it must have been pretty sweet if you thinks you the only one who ever—"

"No, that doesn't matter. What I did was still wrong."

"Takes two."

"I'm not blaming Mr. Young."

"I'm not blaming either one of ya. Just sayin' you might want to enjoy what you got."

"There's nothing between us."

"Coulda fooled me."

"Sonny, I know his reputation. He's a playboy who gets his picture in the paper for going to clubs and yacht parties and all that."

"That lifestyle gets tiring after a while."

"What are you saying?"

"I'm just sayin' don't dismiss anything just yet. Maybe ya met ya match, and I'm sayin' that in a good way."

Maybe Sonny was right. Could she spend her whole life hiding from a tragic past? Rejecting men because of the mistakes of one she'd trusted? What happened tonight with Kelvin could be a signal.

"Now, how late are you planning on stayin' here tonight?"

Lara rose. "I'm leaving, Sonny. Thank you for your kindness."

"Have a good rest tonight, Miss. Those kids are gonna be here tomorrow."

**

Lara opened her eyes, a heavy pit in her stomach. She could barely make out the numbers on her alarm clock. It was just after three.

If Sonny was "in" with Miss Hawthorne, then she and Kelvin would be finished. Even if he didn't tell Hawthorne, he could mention something to Miss Howard and she would go running to Hawthorne.

How long had Sonny worked there? How much influence did Hawthorne exert over him? If he only worked four hours a day, maybe he wasn't on her radar.

Her career was too important for her to take these kinds of risks. If she did anything to jeopardize this position, she'd disappoint herself, her parents, and Dr. Hamilton.

Kelvin is irresistible.

The heat between them shocked her. The chemistry, obvious whenever they were in the same room, hadn't been like anything she'd experienced in her lifetime. Not that she was all that old. But twenty-seven still qualified her as a late bloomer.

He'd brought her to climax twice. Kelvin Young could please and satisfy a woman.

Too bad I need to stay away from men.

Age twelve. Her parents were in one part of the house, Lara and her brother on a different floor. Or in a remote area like the basement or attic. Or, as it had happened the first time, Lara asleep in her bed at night. The room was quiet. A cold winter night. She hadn't heard the door open or her brother, Luke, slip into the room and into her bed. It had started with just his hands.

Although she'd sought therapy, she was guarded and her sessions had done little good. If only she'd opened up in those days, perhaps today would be easier. Perhaps she wouldn't have held back for so long.

It took hours for Lara to fall back asleep, and as soon as she did, her clock radio started blaring. She brewed a strong cup of coffee and had a feeling she was going to need all the strength she could muster today. She rummaged through her closet and returned to a more conservative look. After all, it was the first official day of school. Between new hires' orientation and the professional development days, it was like she had aged a year. She needed to keep herself in check today. She'd do whatever Miss Hawthorne asked of her, as long as Lara didn't feel she was being asked to do someone else's job.

Actually, I already have.

When Lara pulled into the lot, Lewis had his leaf blower fired up, and he was moving a bunch of leaves around. He them out of the way, but no one ever raked and bagged them. That would probably make too much sense.

"Good morning, Mizz Rumson." He sported a broad grin.

"Good morning, Lewis."

Did Sonny tell him already?

Lara shook her paranoia away. She couldn't go through the whole day wondering what people were thinking. Sonny had the late shift and wouldn't be here for hours. He hadn't had time to tell anyone.

"It's nice to have you here, Mizz Rumson. You brighten up the place."

What the hell does he mean by that?

Lara stopped in her tracks. Her face went ashen. She resumed walking, at a much quicker pace.

His comment could mean anything. Maybe he meant she was courteous enough to say hello to him. Most staffers walked by him like he wasn't even there.

As soon as she entered the school, the scent of cinnamon filled the air. She inhaled a sweet fragrance and spotted the cafeteria. She couldn't help but investigate.

A matronly lady placed meal cards in their slots on the wall.

"Good morning. I'm Ms. Rumson, the new vice-principal."

The woman eyed her up and down. "Mrs. Trevor, cafeteria manager."

"What is that wonderful smell?"

"Cinnamon buns for breakfast. Want one?"

"Can't turn that down."

Lara wasn't hungry, but the smell was too good to resist. Mrs. Trevor went into the kitchen and handed Lara a jumbo cinnamon bun wrapped in a paper towel.

"Thank you, Mrs. Trevor."

"Enjoy."

The busses would arrive in about thirty minutes with the kids. She took a bite of her cinnamon bun as she walked to her office. Freshly baked and still warm, and the sweet glaze coated her taste buds. She loved comfort food and this tasty bun was a good way to start this morning.

When she reached her office, she found a stack of papers on her desk. Copies of agendas, class schedules, bell schedules, bus schedules. Was Lara expected to distribute this stuff? That was the secretary's job. Lara scooped up the piles of paper and marched into the office.

Hawthorne was standing by the computer where staff checked in. "Good morning, Ms. Rumson."

"Good morning, Miss Hawthorne, how are you today?"

"I'm doing well, thank you. May I help you with something?"

"I was looking for Miss Jackson."

Miss Hawthorne smiled. "I have her busy with several tasks this morning. She left those on your desk to distribute. She's too busy to do it now."

Lara dumped the stack on Miss Jackson's desk. "Then I guess she'll get to it when she has time. I'll be at my duty station if you need me."

She turned on her heel and walked away, certain Hawthorne's gaze bored into the back of her head.

I gotta do what I gotta do.

Outside, Lara stood in the morning sunshine at her duty station, which entailed monitoring the bus arrivals. When the first bus arrived, she was thrilled to see the children filing off in their crisp pants and school shirts. The colors for Vista Terrace were red and black. The children looked sharp in their uniforms, proudly marching down the breezeway for their first day of the school year. Lara always enjoyed the smiles on their faces on the first day. She only wished those smiles would last.

The morning went relatively well. The students who ate breakfast went to the cafeteria, and those who didn't went to the auditorium. Signs were posted with class rosters for those who had their schedules and tables were set up to distribute schedules to those who had not come to open house last night.

When things quieted down, Lara received word she was to see Miss Hawthorne immediately. Lara was amazed it had taken her this long. She'd been certain Hawthorne would have chewed her out far earlier.

When Lara stepped into Hawthorne's office, the do-nothing counselor sat by her side.

Does Miss Logan have a job or just sit in on meetings?

"Close the door," Miss Hawthorne ordered.

Lara complied and stood before Hawthorne's desk.

"This is a big school. We're in a big school district. Some issues at this school are bigger than me. We help one another here." Miss Hawthorne flung her hand down on the desk with such force it must have stung. Even the counselor appeared to be surprised, although Lara suspected she'd seen this kind of display from Hawthorne before. "I give the orders at Vista Terrace. Me. No one but me is in charge here. When I need something done, I expect to get it done and I don't care who does it."

Lara didn't respond. Hawthorne didn't ask a question, so no response was warranted.

"Now I know you are new here. You're new to the school and to the district. I've tried being flexible with you. Do you understand I'm in charge?"

"Yes, ma'am, and I respect that. I also understand that you seem to resent that Dr. Hamilton went over your head and hired me. If you have an issue with that, perhaps you should take it up with him. If you'd like his number, I can give it to you. If you'll excuse me, I have work to do. Good day."

Lara nodded and bolted from the office, knowing Hawthorne would never call her bluff. As superintendent, Hamilton could fire Hawthorne. Or reassign her to another school, which could make life very unpleasant.

Stand your ground.

Lara hated conflict, and it bothered her that she needed to do this on the first day of school. Had she not done it, the busy work would continue to be shoveled at her left and right. She had to stand up for herself today or the rest of the year would be hell. It still could be, but at least she was not going to be pushed around.

Stand your ground!

**

The young men and women sat in Kelvin's third-period science class. They came prepared and eager to learn, and he was thrilled the year seemed to be off to a good start. Several of them commented on how he was their first male teacher, which struck him as odd. Certainly there had to be others. Strode was new as well, but perhaps Kelvin was the first. It didn't make any sense that a middle school had a largely female staff. In his former school district, the ratio was much more even.

While the students focused on completing a pre-assessment, Kelvin's concentration drifted to Lara. He could still taste her nectar. In fact, he imagined he could still smell it. His face had been plastered with her juices last night. That had been one of the hottest encounters he'd ever had. Finally, he'd broken through her icy exterior and found a desirable woman.

He'd known she had it in her. And he wasn't offended that she'd seemed embarrassed after it was over. Damn, that night custodian must have gotten an earful. He'd brought Lara over the edge twice, and her cries of passion were intense.

Beyond passion.

Drawn to her, he wanted to be with her, but he hoped he hadn't gotten carried away last night.

Of course I did.

How would Lara respond to him today? She'd seemed flustered, but he had caught her off guard. You couldn't plan something like that. He hadn't been able to help himself.

In the classroom. Damn. With Sonny right outside the door. He wanted Lara, but he had to get through to her in a manner other than sexual. She deserved better than that. He couldn't imagine what she must think of him after last night. And what if Sonny talked?

I need to protect her from gossip.

Kelvin wasn't certain if there would be any, but knowing the school system, he'd be surprised if people weren't talking. Lara had a tough enough time with her job; she certainly didn't need any distractions. He had to gain her trust.

At least she wasn't trying to get anything out of him. That set her apart from the others.

"Mr. Young?"

The young woman didn't raise her hand.

"Yes?" Kelvin glanced down at his seating chart. "Sandra."

"Do you believe in Darwin's Theory of Evolution?"

"Why do you ask that?"

"This is science class, isn't it?"

He didn't particularly like her haughty tone. "Yes, it is, but that topic is not part of the curriculum."

"Do you believe that man evolved from apes?"

"That's not something we're covering in this class."

Sandra sat back in her chair. "I'm just curious what your thoughts are." She glared at him. "I'm listening."

There were some uncomfortable giggles from a few others in the class. Kelvin suspected the girl was testing him, and he didn't like where she was going with this. He ignored her and addressed the rest of the class. "When you get your science texts, you can check out the table of contents. It lists all the topics we'll discuss this year."

The bell rang to change classes, and Kelvin breathed easier. Not because he wanted to get rid of his class but because fourth period was his break and he could track down Lara. He needed to see her.

But school wasn't the place to discuss what had happened last night. School wasn't the right place for what they'd done, either, but there was no turning back now. They'd crossed that line. And Kelvin wanted more. He wanted her. But he had to communicate to her that he wasn't all about sex. Or was he?

His reputation wasn't a secret. The things people said

about him and wrote about him. Some of it had elements of truth, other stuff pure nonsense and speculation.

Lara wasn't in her office, so he wandered around the school. He found her dealing with an issue outside of the classrooms and held back, waiting until she was finished. He caught up with her as she walked down the corridor.

"Good morning."

"Good morning." She avoided eye contact.

"How's your day?"

"Fine. Yours?"

"Great! I love my kids."

"I glad you're having a good day."

Kelvin wasn't sure if he should read anything into that or not. Perhaps she wasn't having a good day?

"I'd like to speak with you after school."

"Check with me at the end of the day. I'm needed elsewhere."

Lara picked up her pace down the corridor without ever giving him so much as a glance.

Is she trying to get away from me?

Kelvin needed to talk to her about last night. Or rather, about moving forward from the moments of passion they'd shared. Of course he wanted that, and lots more of it, but he wanted her in other ways as well. He had to make her understand that and hoped she'd be responsive to him.

Kelvin entered the library to search for some books for his classroom. He'd browsed through the textbooks long enough to know they'd bore his kids. Finding material more engaging was always a challenge.

Strode sat on his duff behind one of the computers. Apparently, this must be his planning period as well. Kelvin browsed through the science section. The librarian wasn't anywhere in sight. As he looked through the shelves, he had a feeling he was being watched. It must be Strode. No one else was there. Strode was an odd one and gave Kelvin the creeps.

I want to see Lara.

It was hard to shake her from his mind. Kelvin wanted to know so much more about her. About her background, her family, or her interests outside of school. Those were all important to him. By this time, she probably thought he was nothing more than a sex maniac. His libido went into overdrive every time they were in a room alone together.

How can I tell her I'm more than that?

Kelvin had his wild years when he was in college. Sex was easy and available and he'd taken advantage of it. Many were after him for the Young name, and he'd lost interest in casual sex. He kept to himself and went on an occasional date, but seriously cut down on the indulging. All he wanted was a real, genuine woman.

He recalled the comment that other teacher had made about Lara being an ice queen. Perhaps it was his mission to crack the ice.

I certainly seemed to do that last night.

He found a few books but was not certain of the library's checkout policy, so he waited for the librarian to return. He lingered in the library as far away from Strode as possible.

When the librarian returned, she walked right up to Kelvin. "May I help you, Mr. Strode?"

"It's Mr. Young."

"Oh, I'm sorry. I guess I must have seen Mr. Strode sitting over there when I walked in and his name just stuck in my head."

No need to explain.

"That's fine, may I check these out?"

"Sure, come this way."

As Kelvin left the library, he couldn't shake the feeling that the librarian had called him by Strode's name deliberately.

The remainder of Kelvin's day went well. He enjoyed his classes and enjoyed his students. He had no football coaching commitments today so he was free to leave after the last bell. Lara had seemed a bit distant when he approached her earlier and he decided against tracking her down. Kelvin sent a text.

Can you meet me at 4:00 at Ravens?

No came the response.

Maybe I need to give her some space?

Kelvin shook his head.

Not my style.

He picked up his briefcase and headed to Lara's office. He slipped in and quietly closed the door behind him.

"Hey, how's it going?"

"What do you want?"

"To talk to you. Not here. But we can't ignore it any longer."

Lara's expression became alarmed. "Has anyone said anything?"

"No, of course not. I don't think Sonny's a gossip."

"That would make him the exception." Lara pursed her lips.

"Look, let's just meet off campus for a minute."

"I don't think that's a good idea."

"It's better than me alone with you in your office."

Lara lowered her gaze. "Okay."

"Ravens?"

"Sure."

"I'll be waiting." Kelvin left her alone.

After Kelvin arrived at Ravens and ordered a drink, he didn't have to wait long. Ravens, a low-key lounge, was known as a classy place to unwind. It was quiet, which made it conducive to getting to know someone.

Kelvin selected a comfortable seating area. Two round lounge chairs facing a small round table. Soft jazz filtered unobtrusively through Ravens. It was a little out of the way, on the other side of town but worth it for the ambiance and privacy.

When Lara walked in a short time later, he stood to greet her. She threw her purse down and crossed her legs.

"What can I get you?"

"White wine."

"Chardonnay?"

"Fine."

She's wound up like nothing else.

After Kelvin got her drink, he remained quiet while she took a few sips and unwound from her day. At least, he hoped she did. Working under Miss Hawthorne could wind anyone up.

"How did your day go? Or is that off-limits?"

Lara laughed. It may have been the only time Kelvin had seen her laugh. It was a healthy laugh, and hopefully released some stress.

"Oh, I don't know. It was a day."

Maybe she'd finally let go of that stiff upper lip. Her silky golden hair framed her face and touched her shoulders. She wore a white cotton shirt and blue jeans and carried a simple shoulder bag. Her blouse was unbuttoned enough that he could catch a peek of her creamy breasts. He relished seeing her relaxed and casual. Most of the time, she stressed from the job.

"It's good to hear you laugh. I don't think I've seen you laugh at school."

"You probably never will."

"Do you like the wine?"

"It's perfect, thank you. Just what I need right now."

I know what I need right now.

Getting her out here had seemed like a monumental task. He didn't want to say anything to run her off. He'd have to go slow with her.

"I appreciate you joining me here."

Lara nodded. "It's not too far from my neighborhood. I've been here before. Once." Her blond hair framed her gentle face. He had to break the ice and get her to relax.

Kelvin raised his glass. "If you don't mind my asking a question about work, what do you want to accomplish this year?"

Lara paused. "I want to establish myself as an administrator.

I worked my butt off in the classroom and in my ed leadership program, so now it's time to make it all happen. I just hope I get the opportunity to do so." Lara took another sip of wine.

"Challenges?"

"More than just challenges. Personalities. Feelings. Brick walls."

"Hawthorne's made it that tough for you?"

"Yes, and she serves it up with a smile."

Kelvin nodded. "I'll do whatever I can to protect you."

Lara shook her head. "No, dear, it's my place to protect you. Teachers are easy targets. The year's only just begun. I'm not saying she has anything against you—"

"But"—Kelvin finished her sentence—"I was hired by Hamilton."

"Bingo. Just be careful, Kelvin—I mean Mr. Young."

"You're going to insist on calling me Mr. Young?"

"Yes, I am."

"Then I have no choice but to call you Ms. Rumson."

"No choice at all."

Even in the dim light of the lounge, Kelvin could see her fresh, vibrant face light up with natural beauty. Her subtle makeup made it appear as though she wasn't wearing any.

The iced glass helped quell the heat rising in him. He absently rubbed his other hand against his pants leg. Being with her had him on edge but in a way that excited him.

Challenged him.

He admired her ambition. She'd worked hard to reach vice-principal and probably wanted to go further. They both had obstacles ahead of them, but they would meet those challenges.

"We need to talk about last night." Kelvin hoped he'd given her enough time.

"I know. That's why I agreed to meet you."

"I was wrong to initiate anything on campus, but I couldn't help myself."

Lara leaned back in her chair. "It won't happen again."

"No, you're right. That shouldn't happen at school."

"Kelvin—Mr. Young—it won't happen again at all. I'm an administrator at the school where you teach. We can't continue socializing. Do you know what this could do to our careers?"

"No, I don't."

"Would you date a student?"

"No, of course not."

"I don't mean in middle school. If you taught high school and you were attracted to an eighteen-year-old senior, would you date her?"

"No."

"But it would be legal in Louisiana. It just wouldn't be moral. People would talk, pressure would be put on central administration, and consequences would follow."

Wow. She thought this through.

"I'm not giving up on you. I can respect you not wanting to be seen leaving campus together or meeting during lunch. But I'm going to see you on the weekend."

"Kelvin, you're being—Mr. Young, I mean."

Kelvin chuckled. "See, you can't do it. You can't be formal with me. Not after last night."

"I must be. We must. Don't you value a sense of propriety?"

"You and my mother would get along great. She says that all the time."

Lara looked away.

"Sorry for the jokes. I do take this seriously."

"Then don't tell me. Show me. We work together, that's it."

Kelvin shook his head. "That's not it, Lara. Not anymore."

Lara balled her hand into a fist. "It's Ms. Rumson to you."

"It wasn't Mr. Young last night when you called out my name. You said *Kelvin* more than once."

"You are incorrigible."

"That's another term my mother uses."

"You really don't take this seriously, do you?"

"I take giving us a chance seriously." He met her gaze. Did she understand? Could she pick up on his sincerity?

"There's no us, Kelvin. Why do you keep saying that?" Her voice went soft. Did she believe her own words?

"For the same reason you keep saying Kelvin. Except I'm not denying it."

Her eyes darkened. Lips pursed, then she spoke.

"Kelvin, I have a man problem. I don't do so well with men."

Kelvin hesitated. "You mean you're—"

Lara sighed. "No, I'm not into women. I've just had some problems with men early in my adolescence, and I'm afraid that's clouded my…" Her voice went weak.

"I'm sorry, I didn't mean to pry." Kelvin placed his hand on hers.

She pulled away. "You didn't. I offered the information."

Lara finished her wine. "I'm out of here. Stay out of my office at school. We're not discussing this any further. I'm not killing my career over an indiscretion."

"I'm more than an indiscretion."

Kelvin's heart sank. That cool, frosty front of hers had returned with a vengeance. He lowered his gaze, not wanting her to see the hurt.

CHAPTER SIX

The next morning, Lara fastened her seatbelt. She switched from park to drive but didn't take her foot off the break. Kelvin's words last night kept her frozen in place. *Did he really say he planned on seeing me this weekend?* Her cheeks burned and heart fluttered.

How can he be serious?

Mr. Young had made a career move. A new district. New challenges. Certainly he looked at this assignment as a step up, or he wouldn't have accepted it. He had to take his career seriously. With all his money and the Young name, he didn't need a teacher's income. His intentions had to be in the right place.

So why jeopardize it?

Lara gripped the steering wheel and released the break. Maybe she'd been too hard on Kelvin. After all, he wasn't the only one she had to worry about. She still had no idea if Sonny had said anything. But based on the convo she'd had with him that night, he didn't seem like a gossip.

Sitting next to Kelvin in that lounge had her insides

aching. How could one man be that hot? And why did he have to work in the same school? The longing between her legs when near him signaled danger. It could lead to nothing but more trouble.

Hadn't they caused enough trouble so far? The boss hated them both. They'd performed an indiscretion in a classroom after hours. They'd even shared a kiss during work hours.

This is gonna be a hell of a day.

In order to establish herself as an administrator, she'd stood up to Miss Hawthorne. It was clear to Lara that her boss cared about two things—power and control. Hawthorne would fight her every step of the way. Lara was not about to get stepped on and dumped all over like she was an office clerk.

She arrived at Vista Terrace and pulled into the designated vice-principal parking spot. When she got out of her car, Lewis approached her.

"Good morning, Mizz Rumson."

"Good morning, Lewis." Lara popped her trunk to retrieve some bags.

"Let me help you with that, Mizz Rumson."

"I've got it, Lewis."

"Anything I can do for you this morning?"

"No, thank you, I'm fine."

Why is he being so attentive? What did Sonny tell him?

Lara quickened her step. But Lewis didn't make her uncomfortable. He came across as a good man who meant well. Lara's own insecurity made her uncomfortable—and more than a bit paranoid.

How long before Hawthorne finds out? Or does she know already?

She placed her coffee mug on her cramped desk, dumped her bags on the floor, and logged on to her staff email. There were messages from Hawthorne with assignments. Many of them were administrative but a few were not.

Pick your battles, Rumson.

Her phone chirped from a text. *Have a great day.*

Kelvin. Those big, muscular, dark arms wrapped around her would be a bigger boost. He was a strong man. Those powerful arms had hoisted her feet off the ground when his face was buried in her—

"Good morning, Ms. Rumson."

"Good morning, Miss Hawthorne. How are you today?"

Hawthorne didn't take pleasantries lightly. She expected a formal greeting.

"I'm doing well, thank you. I trust you've checked your email."

"Yes, ma'am, and I'm on it."

"Good. Have a productive day."

Have a productive day.

Not a good day. Not a nice day. A productive day. Lara dived into her tasks. To prove herself, she had to work hard. She wasn't afraid of hard work, as she had worked hard all her life. Perhaps too hard.

She looked away from her computer screen for a moment. Reflecting on the past five years she'd spent in the education system concurrently with pursuing a master's degree, plus the four previous years in college, she'd basically spent a decade of her life working toward her career goals.

And the chemistry between her and Kelvin was undeniable. Her insides tingled and her core ached.

But is it obvious?

Had anyone else besides Sonny noticed? Lara really didn't care what anyone thought, but she did not want it to be a distraction from the job. The attraction between Kelvin and herself could be a detriment if observed by the wrong people.

Perhaps it has been already.

Could she really trust Sonny? Did she have any reason not to? In the two days since it had happened, the only noticeable change was the attention paid to her by Lewis. She doubted Hawthorne knew, but then again, she was a master at putting on a poker face. If she did know, Lara pondered if Hawthorne could somehow use it against her. At this point, Lara wouldn't put anything past her boss. She was clearly drunk on power.

Wrapped up in getting to the work, she had forgotten about her duty. She put down her coffee cup and scurried outside to get to her post on time. As the first bus rolled in, Lara had a sinking feeling that the day had just begun.

"I admire what you did yesterday."

Were those words meant for her? The counselor, Miss Logan, stood next to her. Her back was to Lara. It was as though Miss Logan didn't want to be seen speaking to her.

"Excuse me?" Lara said.

"You stood up to Miss Hawthorne. No one's ever done that before." Miss Logan slipped away.

So…they're all afraid of her.

Later in the office, Lara struggled to pull a jammed piece of paper out of the copy machine while the ladies in the office watched. Her fingers were covered with black toner. The ladies behind the desk sat and did nothing.

"Can anyone help me with this?"

She didn't get a response. They simply averted their gazes and looked elsewhere.

"Good afternoon, Miss Rumson!"

Lara turned to the office doorway, and there stood Dr. Jerrick Hamilton, superintendent of schools.

"Dr. Hamilton. It's good to see you."

He extended his hand.

She blushed. "I'm sorry, I've made a mess."

"I see. Go ahead and wash your hands. I want a tour."

Lara quickly stepped into the restroom. She'd had no idea Hamilton was coming to the campus. She suspected Hawthorne didn't know, either, or else the principal would have expected the staff to put on a dog and pony show. Lara washed her hands and got back to the office in two minutes.

Hawthorne stood there, surprised to see Hamilton.

"I hit as many schools as I could yesterday, and I am trying to get to more today. I'd like you and Miss Rumson to give me a tour of some classrooms."

"Miss Rumson is working," Hawthorne said. "I'll do the walk-through with you."

"Whatever she's doing can wait. I want my principal and my vice-principal to show me around."

Hawthorne's lips tightened. Awkward, but at the same time, Hamilton bolstered Lara's confidence.

"Right this way." Hawthorne led the way out of the office.

As they walked down the corridor, Lara took some satisfaction in imagining how uncomfortable Hawthorne must be feeling. Hamilton was the top boss, but Hawthorne resented his changes. Lara smirked.

This is going to be interesting.

Hawthorne led them down one of the corridors and opened a classroom door. "This is Ms. Ord's eighth grade language arts class. She's tight with discipline and her class reflects it." Hawthorne spoke in a quiet voice so as not to disturb the class. Hamilton nodded. The principal gently closed the door and moved on.

Pausing before another door, Hawthorne faced Hamilton. "This is Mr. Strode. He teaches seventh grade math and is our boys' basketball coach." Hawthorne opened the door. Strode was sitting at his desk and the class was not engaged. They appeared to be hanging out. Lara began to tense. This was the last thing any principal wanted a supervisor to see.

Hawthorne quickly shut the door. "Next door is your Mr. Young. Eighth grade science and football." Hawthorne opened Kelvin's classroom door.

Did she just say your? Who's she talking to, Hamilton or me?

Kelvin was on his feet teaching and his class was engaged. Lara smiled. This was exactly what an administrator should see.

"Now that's more like it," Hamilton said.

Lara glanced at Hawthorne but couldn't read her expression.

"Shall we continue?" Hawthorne asked.

Lara was proud of Kelvin. He was a shining example of what a good teacher should be, and Hamilton had seen it. She would die to know how Hawthorne felt right now. She suppressed a chuckle.

"You've done very well. Congratulations for getting off to a good start, Hawthorne." Dr. Hamilton was being polite. Strode's class had been a mess. Hawthorne would probably hear about that privately.

"Have you seen enough, Dr. Hamilton?" Hawthorne sounded like she wanted this tour to end.

"Yes, I need to get to another school today. Miss Rumson, Miss Hawthorne, I thank you for your time. I can find my way out."

Lara wished Hamilton hadn't left her standing there with Hawthorne. The air between them grew thick. They both moved in the direction of the office, but neither of them said a word. Lara wanted to say something but couldn't think of an appropriate comment. Finally, after a walk down the corridor, which seemed to last forever, they reached the office.

"I'll get right back to what I was doing, Miss Hawthorne."

Hawthorne didn't acknowledge her but disappeared into the office.

Lara smiled, satisfied after Hamilton's impromptu visit. The superintendent had seen the real Vista Terrace. A hardworking new hire like Kelvin and an older, stodgy, set-in-his-ways do-nothing like Mr. Strode. Lara suspected Hamilton had seen exactly what he'd expected to see.

She finished the job at the copy machine—which none of the office ladies had touched in her absence—and returned to her computer. She received an email from Miss Hawthorne. *Mr. Strode is not getting the instructional support he needs. Please provide him with some early finisher activities.*

Amazingly, Hawthorne had found a way to make Strode's laziness Lara's fault. Not a problem. She had dozens of early finisher activities on her junk drive. She'd dump those on Strode and be good to go. Lara busied herself with selecting the materials. It would probably be a good idea to try to please Hawthorne today. No doubt she still simmered from Hamilton's visit and would most likely be in a foul mood for the remainder of the day.

Lara couldn't resist. She pulled her phone from her handbag and sent Kelvin a text. *You were awesome today.* After collecting her materials, she headed back to the copy machine to finish the job for Strode. She didn't like making copies in the main office. The ladies who worked there always seemed to be staring at her. Could they resent her as well? She had done nothing to offend them, so perhaps they were just following Hawthorne's example.

Having made her copies, Lara strolled down the corridor to Strode's room with a stack of papers in her arm. When she turned the corner, she could have sworn Strode had stepped out of the custodian's utility closet. It could have been the men's room if there was one right next to it. She wasn't close enough to be sure after all.

Was he talking to Sonny?

No, Sonny didn't come into work until much later.

Strode reached his door just ahead of her and closed it almost in her face. Lara was tempted to drop the stack of papers on the floor but decided to be professional about it and knock. Strode opened the door and looked at her as though she were a bruise on an apple.

"Miss Hawthorne asked me to give you these." Lara thrust the papers toward him and left quickly so he didn't have a chance to speak. She didn't wait for Strode to ask what they were or even say thank you. He left her with a creepy feeling, and she wanted to get away from him.

It wasn't until Lara turned down the next corridor that it occurred to her that this was not Strode's break time.

What was he doing out of the room?

Perhaps an aide watched his class so he could step out to use the restroom. But she hadn't seen an aide in the room and didn't really care. The man was strange.

Footsteps sounded behind her. Lara turned around. It was Lewis, his face ashen, as though he were ill.

"Are you okay, Mr. Lewis?"

He shook his head, answered, "Fine," and continued down the hall at a brisk pace.

What's up with him?

Vista Terrace had quite a cast of characters. Lara's old school was nothing like this. She had a lot to get used to.

Lara reflected on Hawthorne's email. It made no mention of Ms. Ord or Kelvin. Was that a good thing or not? Hamilton had left on a positive note, so surely Hawthorne took some comfort in that. Lara didn't envy her boss right now. Strode was a blemish on an otherwise positive walk-through.

Hawthorne could try to pin it on Lara, but Hamilton was smart enough to know what was going on or not going on in a classroom. That was a reflection of the principal since the buck stopped with Hawthorne.

After the children were dismissed for the day, Lara was called to the office.

"Miss Hawthorne had to go to a meeting at the school board. There's a parent here who wants to speak to someone." The secretary nodded to the woman seated on the bench with two girls.

Lara assumed her title as vice-principal made her *someone*. She nodded to the secretary, then walked over to the parent and extended her hand.

"I'm Lara Rumson, vice-principal."

"Bridget Cartwright."

Lara couldn't invite this woman into her sad excuse for an office. She turned to the secretary.

"Is there a conference room?"

"They use Miss Logan's office. She went with Miss Hawthorne to the meeting, so it's probably locked. I'll page a custodian to open it."

"Thank you." Lara turned to Mrs. Cartwright. "This way, please."

She took a good look at Mrs. Cartwright as she gathered up her bag and two children. She appeared to be about ten years older than Lara, with perfectly coiffed hair. Her salon highlights were held in place with plenty of hair spray. Her makeup must be time-consuming to apply. She wore a burgundy turtleneck top with a silver brooch and camel slacks. The Coach bag matched her outfit.

When they reached Miss Logan's office, the door was already unlocked.

"What can I do for you, Mrs. Cartwright?" Lara asked as she gestured for them to sit.

"This is my daughter Sandra. She's in the eighth grade. And this is Brandy, she's in the sixth grade." Mrs. Cartwright beamed at her daughters.

Lara managed a smile.

"I wanted to know what other options were available for Sandra's science class."

"Is there a problem?" Lara turned to Sandra, who didn't respond.

"No, there's no problem," Mrs. Cartwright said. "We'd just like to know what other classes are available."

"Science is a required subject. She can't opt out of it if that's what you mean."

"No, I know she needs to take science. I'm just asking if there are other classes."

Lara turned to Sandra. "Who's your science teacher?"

"Mr. Young."

"It's only the second day of school. Why do you want to switch classes?"

Sandra shrugged.

Mrs. Cartwright opened her mouth as though to speak, but Lara jumped in with another question. "Is someone in the class bothering you, Sandra?"

Sandra shook her head.

"Can you tell me what I can do to help you?"

Sandra was silent. Mrs. Cartwright cleared her throat.

"Since Sandra is here," Lara said, "I'd rather hear it from her." She turned her attention back to Sandra. "If you're asking to switch classes, Sandra, I need to hear a reason. Otherwise, I can't consider moving you."

Sandra looked away, uncomfortable. Lara got the impression this had to do more with the mother.

"Mrs. Cartwright, can you tell me why Sandra should be moved?"

"I didn't mean to suggest she should be moved; I was simply asking if there were any other options."

"Okay, I respect that, Mrs. Cartwright. Yes, there are other science classes if that answers your question."

There was an awkward silence. Mrs. Cartwright looked at her children. Sandra looked away, while Brandy appeared disinterested.

"So," Mrs. Cartwright said, "if Sandra wanted a class reassignment…"

"She would need to present me with a compelling reason." Lara looked into Mrs. Cartwright's sapphire blue eyes.

"Mr. Young is new to the district."

Lara nodded. "Yes, he is. And?"

"He hasn't really been teaching all that long."

"Eight years."

"Well, I saw Mr. Young at open house."

"Did you speak with him?"

"No, we didn't. We were anxious to meet Brandy's teachers since this is her first year at Vista Terrace."

Lara could see where this was going. Mrs. Old Money Cartwright had seen a black man at open house and found out he was her daughter's teacher. Lara stood up and extended her hand. "Thank you so much for your time, Mrs. Cartwright. Your children are in very good hands with the teachers at Vista Terrace. Enjoy the rest of your day. I'll walk you out, then I have to return to work."

She breathed easier when they left. So, this was what administrators had to deal with. Picky parents.

She had some work to finish up but didn't think it would take long. This day had been tense. After Dr. Hamilton left, Miss Hawthorne's sour mood had hovered over the school for the rest of the day.

Lara sat at her desk entering some schedule changes onto the school server when Sonny showed up. He emptied her trash, and it appeared to take him quite a long time to do it.

"Good afternoon, Sonny."

"Good afternoon, Ms. Rumson. How was your day?"

"I got through it, Sonny." Lara smiled.

Sonny returned the smile, although it was more of a grin that lingered.

"How are you, Sonny?"

"Doin' just fine, ma'am. My day going just fine."

She nodded.

"You put in some pretty late hours yourself, ma'am," Sonny said.

Is he making reference to…?

Lara bristled. "Not every day."

Sonny was a tall man, probably about forty. He had some battle scars on his face. She didn't know much about him, but he might have been in some fights when he was young.

When he spoke to Lara, he was polite, although he held his gaze on her a bit too long.

"You working late tonight, miss?"

"No, Sonny, I'm trying to finish up so I can get out of here."

"Anything I can do for you?"

Lara wasn't sure how to respond. She couldn't read anything into his tone.

"I'm fine."

"Well, if you need the floor mopped or anything like that, you just let me know and I'll take care of it."

"Thank you, Sonny."

"I'd rather you just tell me what you need rather than going to Lewis or the boss. Just tell me what you need done, and I'll take care of it for you."

"I appreciate that."

"Good day, Miss."

Lara picked up a document off her desk but didn't read it. Tension crept up her neck. Sonny was just being courteous. There was no reason to feel uncomfortable around him. He hadn't done or said anything inappropriate.

But Lara's behavior with Kelvin was inappropriate—at work.

Could Sonny do something to blackmail them?

CHAPTER SEVEN

It was expected that students challenged a new teacher. Kelvin figured that would happen after switching to a new school in another district. The students of Vista Terrace didn't disappoint.

"Do you have a question?" Kelvin asked.

"Huh?" the student said.

"You heard me."

"No."

"Then why are you talking?"

"I wasn't talking."

Kelvin was used to this kind of exchange. He had been through it dozens of times with students. They all played the same games, although this crowd seemed to be a tougher audience than usual.

"What are we gonna do in this class anyway?"

Kelvin turned in the student's direction. It was Sandra, the same girl who'd given him a hard time yesterday. She appeared to be studying him.

"That's a good question, Sandra. We're going to go over the unit guide right now."

Sandra rolled her eyes.

"Do you have a problem with something I just said?" Kelvin met her glare.

"No, Mr. Young." Her voice dripped with sarcasm.

Why does she have a problem with me?

Kelvin exhaled when the fourth period bell rang. It had been a rough morning. The kids were mainly on their best behavior day one, and the real deal started to show through on day two. They challenged him every step of the way. Kelvin could handle challenges, but it was tough getting through that bumpy attitude adjustment period.

He strolled down the hall to get out of the classroom for a minute. He passed Strode's room. Strode, seated at his desk, engaged in conversation on his mobile phone. What were those airs really about? Strode was a loner and didn't appear to speak to anyone else on campus, but he wasn't shy. He appeared more arrogant than anything.

Kelvin hoped to run in to Lara, just to get a glimpse of her beautiful behind, but he wasn't being realistic. After what had happened at open house, it would be wise to avoid any unnecessary contact. He had the weekend to look forward to.

He considered inviting Lara down to his place that long drive might be too much for a first date. It seemed odd to even call it that. Reservations at a nice restaurant would be a more realistic option. At a high-end spot where they wouldn't be bothered by nosy colleagues. Kelvin wanted Lara relaxed… completely relaxed.

Kelvin couldn't resist. He pulled out his cell phone and sent her a text. *How is your day going?*

"Good afternoon, Mr. Young."

Kelvin nodded to Ms. Howard. "Good afternoon." Due to her reputation as a gossip, he kept his distance from her. A pleasantry here and there, but he gave her nothing more. He continued down the corridor without so much as a pause, headed toward the library.

Kelvin was in the library for only a short time when he was summoned to Miss Hawthorne's office.

What now?

She was seated behind her desk, with the counselor perched on a chair next to her.

Does the counselor do anything at this school?

"You wanted to see me, ma'am?" Kelvin stood in the doorway. He didn't dare enter until invited.

"Yes, Mr. Young, come on in, and close the door."

Close the door?

He did as Miss Hawthorne instructed and stood next to a chair.

Miss Hawthorne nodded. "Have a seat."

Kelvin sat down. The counselor's glance drop to her lap.

"We have a policy at Vista Terrace that prohibits the use of mobile phones on campus. This applies to the staff as well as the students. I appreciate that you're new here, Mr. Young, so I'm going to consider this to be a verbal warning. The next time it happens, there will be a write-up. Is that clear?"

"Yes, ma'am."

"You may go."

Wow. So it has begun.

Kelvin had known it was only a matter of time before he became a target. Lara had essentially warned him. She was the easy target since she had to work so closely with Miss Hawthorne. Apparently, his time had come.

Lara probably got it tenfold but being professional she didn't let it show. Since Lara was an administrator, Hawthorne must give it to her hard. A vice-principal was a direct threat to Hawthorne's job. Kelvin, as a teacher and coach, posed no threat.

Outsiders didn't appear to be welcome in this district. People nodded and smiled, but no one reached out to him or offered any help. Kelvin could take care of himself, but he found the people in this school district odd. Characters like Strode seemed to be the norm here.

Kelvin headed for the weight room. He needed to work off some tension, and that would be the most realistic way to do it. Of course, with Lara, he could think of better ways to release tension, but that would have to wait.

Fortunately, the weight room was empty. Kelvin did his stretching routine relieved the room was so quiet. Threats of a write-up drifted away, and more comforting images of Lara filled his mind. He needed to see her.

**

Kelvin loved after-school football practice. He had a strong group of seventh and eighth grade boys on his team. He took a great deal of pride in seeing his boys work hard. While coaching, Kelvin was in his element.

He baked in the hot Louisiana sun, and marveled at how

his boys did it. They wore heavy football gear, and not one of them complained. Perspiration drenched their faces and seeped through their clothing.

"Water break!" Kelvin shouted.

They lined up single file and removed chilled bottled water from the cheap plastic coolers that had Vista Terrace scrawled on them with marker. They smiled as they passed him, and Kelvin couldn't give them enough praise.

"You're doing a great job. You're all showing me the best you can be."

The neighborhood was scattered with a contrast of middle-class houses and poorer developments, so he could only speculate what they had to go home to. Here, they shined.

"Coach, how much longer?" DaShon was a seventh grader. Sixth graders were not allowed on the team, so this was his first year playing. When Kelvin looked into DaShon's eyes, some of himself reflected back. Idealistic. Enthusiastic. A young man with a future. The only difference, DaShon would have to leap over many more hurdles, beginning with this neighborhood.

Nothing prevented Kelvin from bonding with them. His chest swelled. He'd accomplished so much in eight years of teaching and coaching.

Kelvin smiled. "You bored?"

"No, sir."

"You tired?"

"No, sir."

"Then never ask how much longer, DaShon. It gives the impression you don't want to be here."

DaShon shook his head and flashed a smile. "Nah, it's not that, coach. I just gotta go to work."

"You're not old enough to work." Kelvin doubted he needed the reminder.

"Help my uncle with stuff around his yard. Gotta try to get it done before it gets dark."

"I understand that, but we're going to finish practice before I release you. It's still early... You'll have plenty of daylight left."

DaShon gave him the peace sign. One advantage of middle school was that it started early and released early. It gave him and his boys plenty of time for practice and they could still do their homework or whatever at night.

Vista Terrace had quite a few after-school athletics programs. Miss Hawthorne had a competitive spirit. Kelvin suspected she supported the programs because she liked winning. His mission was different. He had a vision for strong, successful young men and women in and outside of the classroom.

"Good afternoon, Mr. Young." Dr. Hamilton approached with a thirty-something man with broad shoulders.

"Dr. Hamilton." Kelvin extended his hand.

"I want you to meet Devon Jackson, the football coach at Grayson High School. He'll be keeping an eye on your eighth grader players this year."

"Kelvin Young."

Mr. Jackson shook his hand. "Good to meet you. I'm not going to keep you from your practice. Just wanted to match a name with the face."

Face with the name.

"Keep up the good work, Mr. Young." Hamilton led Jackson away from the playing field.

Kelvin wasn't sure what to make of that. How would a high school football coach have time in his day to scope out the eighth graders? Jackson might attend a game or two, but Kelvin doubted he'd be seeing much of him.

Someone lurked around the bleachers, and Kelvin had to squint in the sunlight to see. It was Strode.

What's he doing here?

Kelvin no longer attempted any pleasantries with Strode. He was probably another one of Hawthorne's spies, along with Miss Howard. He seemed like one of those types who would have Hawthorne's ear, but Kelvin couldn't care less. He wasn't here to bother with pettiness.

He focused his attention on coaching these fine young men. With his guidance, they would become successful not only in football but also with their academics. Kevin had played college football, but his desire to teach had prevented him from pursuing the game on a professional level. He enjoyed what he did now.

After he got the last of the boys on the late bus, he headed back to his room to pack up. Sonny swept the corridor right outside his door.

"'Sup, Mr. Young?"

Kelvin bristled at *'sup.* It implied a familiarity he didn't have with Sonny.

"Good evening, Sonny," Kelvin said.

"Workin' another late one, Mr. Young?"

Kelvin's eyes shifted away from Sonny. Unlocking his door, he said, "You know I coach, Sonny."

He shut the door before Sonny could toy with him any further. The custodian obviously had knowledge he and Lara had shared a sexual moment in the classroom after the open house. Lara's whimpering and moaning when she climaxed were clear indicators. What he didn't know was how many people Sonny had told, if any.

Kelvin walked down the corridor to leave. Strode's light was on, but he couldn't determine if Strode was in the room. He doubted he was working. Strode barely did a thing during the day.

There's no basketball practice today. What's he doing here?

Kelvin continued to his car, trying to shake away the odd sighting at Vista Terrace. Except his sightings of Lara. He wanted her and he had to convince her he was for real. He had let his hormones rage out of control with her several times. Now, he had to make her understand his sincerity. This weekend he would do just that.

Those stolen moments at school were nothing compared to how he wanted to make love to her. Lara evoked a desire in him. Her beauty, her poise, and her indifference to his wealth aroused him. For a change, he was pursuing a woman he wanted instead of politely rebuffing the gold diggers. He liked it this way. Lara represented a challenge and he needed a good, strong woman in his life.

And with the weekend coming up, he had to devise a plan.

CHAPTER EIGHT

Lara stared at her phone as though it were something alien. Had she really just allowed Kelvin Young to talk her into a date this weekend? Seriously? She must be going insane.

They couldn't. They worked together, with Kelvin being subordinate to her. Didn't Louisiana have abuse of power laws? She couldn't remember if that was covered in her educational leadership curriculum. Those years she'd worked on her master's and taught full time were all a blur. She'd never worked so hard in her life.

Although, Hawthorne seemed determined to match that and then some.

If nothing else, Kelvin certainly was persistent. He wouldn't take no for an answer. Lara ticked through her possibilities. Cancel. Cite conflict of interest. Go through with it and behave like a psycho to scare him off. Or go and have a great time.

No, it wouldn't work.

Frigid's my middle name.

The words of a stranger came back to haunt her. *She's an*

ice queen. But what had Lara said or done to give the teacher that impression? Lara couldn't recall saying or doing anything, so it must have been demeanor.

Frankly, she'd struggled with that for years. Her defense mechanism. Ever since she'd tried to put her life back together after the repeated molestations, she couldn't move past them. Until she'd met Kelvin Young. But why? There had to be more to it than that.

If that was the case, getting to know Kelvin better would do no harm. It seemed like it might help. Finally get past years of repressed emotions and denial. Something she'd tried but failed to do.

Besides, it was just a date. He'd invited her to dinner. What harm could there be in that? She had gone out for a drink with him the other night, which she hadn't planned on doing.

Looks weren't all that. He just happened to be irresistible. Social media presented him as cavalier, and he was anything but. He'd always been respectful to her at school and dealt with the pressures of working under Hawthorne. A less seasoned teacher might have cracked, but he held up well.

No need worrying about it. Dinner. Have a few laughs, maybe. Call it a night. And hopefully, avoid talking about Vista Terrace.

But people would still talk if someone found out about them. Above all, they had to maintain discretion. She still fretted over Sonny. From what she'd learned about public education in her career so far, everyone gossiped. Some did more so than others, of course.

Tumbleweeds rolled through her stomach. So much for staying calm and not worrying.

At least the remainder of the week went without incident.

On Friday, Kelvin sent her a text message. *I'll pick you up at 7:15.*

She raised an eyebrow over Kelvin's text. Gallant of him, since Lara fully expected to drive herself to the date.

It had been a long day, but all things said, a relatively quiet one. She'd put out the occasional fire here and there. Nothing out of the ordinary had happened, and the children were pumped up because today was Friday.

Lara sat in her depressing office and filled out end of the week reports for Miss Hawthorne. Being a vice-principal came with a lot of paperwork. Miss Hawthorne wanted them done online but requested a hard copy as well. That meant Lara had to fight with a printer that always jammed. Welcome to public education.

"Empty your trash, Miss?"

Something was different about Sonny. Before the open house night, Sonny would simply grab her trash can and toss it without saying a word. He might nod, but that was about it. Now, he often tried to engage her in conversation.

"Thank you." Lara didn't meet his gaze. She didn't need Sonny getting too familiar with her. He was a thin man, missing a tooth or two. He still had a reasonably good smile, though, and he always appeared well groomed.

"Any plans for the weekend, Miss?"

Lara glanced at Sonny, and as she did, he adjusted something around his pants pocket. She glimpsed the outline of something the size of a French bread before she glanced away.

"None." She got up, rushed past him, and bolted for the printer.

Oh, no, he didn't.

But he did. She was certain he had just adjusted his cock. She didn't know if he'd done it intentionally or as a matter of habit, but it didn't matter. The bottom line was she couldn't say anything. Not after what Sonny had seen—or rather, heard.

Lara peered into the printer output tray. Amazingly, her pages had printed without jamming. But this was only one report. She needed to go back to her office and finish the rest. By the time she got there, Sonny was gone.

What does he want?

Lara needed to put him out of her mind, focus on getting home, and prepare for her date with Kelvin.

A date I shouldn't be having.

Lara typed away, entered data, and finished up her work for the week.

It was unusual for Hawthorne to leave campus early, but her door was locked, and the office staff was gone.

It's Friday.

Lara placed the hard copies on the secretary's desk and left a big note on top of the stack indicating they were for Miss Hawthorne.

Lara returned to her office and sent Hawthorne an email outlining what she'd completed. That way, Lara was covering her tracks should her stack of papers get misplaced.

She breathed a sigh of relief when she finally got out of

there. Her workweek was finished—at least on the clock—and she could focus on her weekend. The mountain of work Hawthorne had given Lara could wait. She craved a relaxing shower and planned on taking one as soon as she got home. It was a gorgeous afternoon about to be evening, and the breeze against her face invigorated her as she drove.

What if someone sees us?

She'd taken that risk the other night, but wasn't that just to get rid of him? How had he talked her into yet another date? Or was that a date? No question how she'd allowed it to happen. His charm couldn't be denied.

And his masculine allure.

Under a hot shower, she recalled Kelvin's text about picking her up. Shouldn't they go in separate cars? Or was she being paranoid? After grabbing a shower puff, she lathered up with body wash and inhaled the vanilla-peach scent of the body wash. Streams of water slowly rinsed the lather away.

In a robe and slippers, Lara sauntered into the kitchen and opened a bottle of chilled Riesling. She poured a glass and retreated into the bedroom to apply makeup and get dressed.

Lara rummaged through her closet and selected the black cotton Gianfranco Ferrè cocktail dress. Some would say it was too hot to wear black, but she'd fit in fine with the more upscale crowd at Calvin's. The cut of the shoulder area made her appear taller, and it contrasted nicely with her blond hair.

Her phone rang. It was still in her purse where she'd

dumped her stuff earlier. Lara managed to reach it before it went to voice mail.

"Hello?"

"Is it okay if I stop by early? I'm here." His smooth, seductive voice sent chills through her. A man with a voice like that could make her agree to almost anything.

Lara glanced at the clock. He was fifteen minutes early.

Courteous of him to call.

"Sure, Kelvin, come on up."

What did I just do?

Inviting him into her home wasn't on the agenda. But she hadn't completely dressed yet, and she couldn't very well leave him out in the heat. She quickly scrambled to pick up all the unread paperbacks littering her living room floor. Gee, an effort should have been made to clean up sooner, huh?

Lara poured a glass of wine for Kelvin and set it by the couch. She opened her door just as he strolled down the hallway.

"Evening!" His smile captivated her as it had the day they'd met.

"Come on in."

"How are you feeling?" His deep, dark eyes expressed concern.

"Terrific. I poured you some wine. I'll be ready in a minute, as soon as I can find some shoes."

Lara returned to the bedroom, which gave her a minute to collect herself. Still nervous, she had to go through with this. Had to see if it was possible to be with a man, for her sake, nothing else.

He smells good.

Lara poked through her collection for a suitable pair of

shoes and found just the right heel height. She ran a brush through her hair, double-checked her makeup, and sprayed on a dash of perfume. Despite her reservations, she was ready to face the evening.

When Lara returned to the living room, Kelvin grinned. "You look amazing."

His paper-white teeth sparkled. Dressed in a pressed pair of black slacks and a charcoal-gray shirt, he was beautiful.

Lara sat down next to him for a moment.

"This is good wine," Kelvin said.

"Thank you. I discovered German wines on a trip one summer, and I've enjoyed them ever since."

"Are you ready for seafood at Calvin's?"

"Yes. Seafood is one of my favorites."

"How was your day?"

"Busy. I managed to keep out of the way and get my work done."

Kelvin put his wine down. "Okay, enough about work. Let's eat."

"I'll drink to that." Lara took one more sip, then placed her glass down.

Pangs of unease shot through her. If Hawthorne found out her vice-principal was fraternizing with a teacher, her career could be harmed. But how could Hawthorne find out?

Calvin's wasn't far from Lara's place, yet it was out of the way enough that they shouldn't run into any Vista Terrace staff. Calvin's catered more to the old-money crowd, which Portsmith had plenty of. Lara's parents descended from old money, and Kelvin's family, although not in Portsmith, went way back with their wealth.

When they entered, the maitre d' greeted Kelvin warmly. They appeared to know one another. There were quite a few people waiting, yet Kelvin and Lara were immediately escorted to a table. Lara didn't expect to see it crowded so early. The maitre d' held her chair for her and placed a napkin on her lap.

"Thank you, Charles," Kelvin said.

So they do know one another.

Charles handed the wine list to Kelvin. He studied the list until he pointed to something. Charles nodded and took the list from him.

Lara glanced around, still nervous. Not a familiar face in sight, at least not anyone from the school district. If she planned on enjoying the evening, forget about anyone else. But Kelvin.

"We can both use tonight's celebration."

"Celebration?"

"We survived our first week at Vista Terrace."

Lara shot him a glare.

Kelvin shook his head. "I did it again."

"Last time," Lara said.

Kelvin threw his hands up. "Okay, I promise. No more mention of work."

"I've heard that before."

"I'll change the subject. You have a very nice condo."

"Thank you."

"How long have you had it?"

"Since I got my bachelor's degree—a bit more than five years."

The sommelier arrived with the wine. He went through his ritual, Kelvin nodded his approval, and in a moment, they were raising their glasses.

And that was she froze.

Across the room, his profile to their table, sat a man resembling that oddball Mr. Strode. Could it be him? She couldn't tell if he was tall enough to be Strode since he was seated.

Better not say anything to Kelvin. He'd say it was just paranoia, and he'd probably be right. Lara took a healthy sip of her wine and placed her glass down.

Is Strode in with Hawthorne?

"How is it?" Kelvin asked.

"Lovely." Lara would much rather look at Kelvin. He was far more attractive than the gangly stranger.

"I chose it based on your tastes."

"I thought so." Lara sniffed her glass. "I appreciate the continuity from the bottle I opened at home. But this one's better."

And what the hell was she doing gazing around the restaurant when a gorgeous man sat across from her?

Lara admired Kelvin's attention to detail. He made a striking impression with his class. And did it so effortlessly. He must have been raised well.

She'd been as well. She had a good career, a comfortable condo, and the support of a good family. Her parents were always there when she needed them, without exception. She longed for the day when she could make them proud and pay them back.

Making them proud is paying them back.

Lara's ambition eclipsed her personal life. Now, could it be the time to find some balance? For the first time in years, perhaps in her life, was she ready to seriously explore those possibilities? Surprised by the trust she placed in Kelvin so far, and the comfort level she had with him, she also found it exhilarating. His intensity left her yearning for more of his good company.

"Do you spend much time with your family?" Kelvin asked.

"I do." The question caught Lara off guard. She didn't recall Kelvin asking about her family before. "I see them most weekends. They don't live too far from Portsmith."

Since Kelvin came from a wealthy family, she'd assumed he was tired of women asking about them. She chose to allow him to steer the conversation as long as the topic remained on family.

"Do they have big gatherings on the holidays?"

Lara laughed. "Oh, do they ever. They love to entertain."

She glanced across the room at the stranger, dining alone. It wasn't Strode, she was certain of that now. She'd been silly at best.

Can I forget about that nonsense and concentrate on Kelvin?

CHAPTER NINE

When Lara led Kelvin up the stairs of her condo, she was certain her snoopy downstairs neighbor peered out her window at them.

Not that Lara had any gossip. She kept to herself, went to work, came back home.

"Please, sit down." Lara gestured to the sofa before she disappeared into the bathroom.

When she finished, she tried to find an appropriate dessert wine to serve Kelvin. Port. She had a bottle of that somewhere. It had been a gift from an aunt. A condo-warming gift if Lara remembered accurately, which meant the thing had sat there for years.

Dinner had gone quite well. She'd enjoyed Kelvin's conversation, and she'd been able to shake off her apprehension and have a good time.

"Here we are." Lara stepped into the living room carrying a large tray holding the bottle, two glasses, and an arrangement of aged goat cheese with crackers.

"Let me help you with that." Kelvin took the tray from

her hands and set it down on the coffee table.

"Thank you."

Lara poured them both a glass of port. The golden-brown color of the tawny wine reflected nicely from the candle on the table. Lara leaned back on the couch and let out a deep breath.

"Feeling good?"

"Feeling somewhat okay. Still a bit jittery."

"Why?"

Lara shifted in her seat. "Same worries. Us fraternizing." But it was more than that. What happened in her youth still haunted her. She'd hinted at it in the restaurant.

Should I tell him?

"I believe those concerns only apply to teachers and students, Lara. And you probably know that since you got your admin certification."

Her heart leaped. Of course he was right. Although no law existed, it still didn't mean it couldn't be used against them.

"It's more than that." Lara's palpitations increased. "I told you earlier I wasn't so good with men."

Kelvin shrugged. "Everyone's different. I don't see that as a problem."

"It has been a problem. For me. It's like there's a barrier between me and men. Or, at least, between me and intimacy."

"Do you know where that comes from?" Kelvin put his hand on hers. "If you don't mind my asking."

"Not at all. I brought it up." Lara took a deep breath. Talking about it wasn't enough. She could tell Kelvin, but she'd be making excuses for herself instead of taking action.

But if she didn't tell him, then she'd deny him the chance to understand her better. He'd been nothing but honest with her. Kind. Generous with his attention.

No, there'd be no talking about it. She had to let go and experience a man for her own pleasure.

Lara shook her head. "I'm being silly, that's what it's all about. I'm holding on to thoughts I should have abandoned long ago."

"You need to let go of those thoughts." Kelvin leaned forward. "And enjoy the evening."

"I agree." Lara nodded. "Thank you again for dinner. I can't recall having such good seafood."

"I'm glad you liked it. Calvin's doesn't disappoint."

"Kelvin doesn't disappoint." Lara surprised herself with her boldness. The loaded statement could be interpreted in more than one way. Kelvin gazed into her eyes, and Lara placed a hand on his arm.

He put his glass down and moved closer to her. He pressed his lips against hers, and his powerful arms wrapped around her. Lara opened her mouth to welcome his tongue.

The weight of the week, the stress and the frustration, evaporated from her body. For once in her life, she willingly surrendered to the desire building inside. The years of repression didn't seem to matter right now.

He'd captivated her in a way she hadn't known possible. It became clear why romance had eluded her all these years. She hadn't met Kelvin Young.

His lips moved to her throat, and Lara gasped. Jolts of

pleasure sparked through her and her pulse raced. She grabbed the back of his head, and his tongue glided along her nape. She closed her eyes and shivered from the tingling sensation moving through her body.

A simple kiss. That was all she'd allow. If she could let him kiss her at school, she could certainly submit to a goodnight kiss here. But nothing about Kelvin indicated he was saying good night.

"Kelvin…"

His lips glided along the other side of her neck. She let out a soft giggle as his tongue tickled her. Oh, if the tingling in her body told her anything, it was that the night had just begun.

"Kiss me." Speaking those words surprised her. She'd never asked a man to do that. But the ache between her legs served as her cue.

Embrace the moment.

Kelvin obeyed, and her tongue hungered for his. Warmth permeated through her belly, and she put both her arms around him to hold him close.

He hoisted her up off the couch.

Lara became dizzy for a moment as he moved from left to right.

What's he doing?

Her body floated across the room until he laid her down on her back. He'd found her bedroom.

Kelvin moved on top of her, and his large, muscular frame hovered over her body. It was the first time she was on her back looking up at him, and he was like something out of a dream. She couldn't see much in the room with only the hallway light spilling in, but his strong presence was overpowering.

"Are you okay?" Kelvin asked.

Lara nodded. Her emotions pinged in all directions, but her body only wanted him. She shivered, about to cross a line she hadn't willingly crossed with a man. With Kelvin, the time had come.

Or had it? Fear spiked through her, mixed with raw lust. Would she regret it? Or would it be a step she'd put off too long in her own healing? Those nights that Luke had snuck into her room. The pain. The silent screams. The uncleanliness of it all. Shame. Guilt. Powerlessness. She couldn't fight with conflicting feelings the rest of her life.

Move forward.

Kelvin's lips pressed against hers, and the fear melted away. Lara's hand rested against the waves in his hair, holding him to her. Fire raged in her core as she probed his mouth with her tongue, tasting a hint of port. The alcohol had cleansed his palette, leaving no trace of dinner.

He kissed her, and his hands moved up to her breasts, squeezing them. She'd been blessed with a more than ample bosom, and his hands were so large they practically engulfed her globes. Kelvin's thumbs swirled over her swollen nipples.

The heat in her belly surged. She'd taken that step and didn't dare turn back.

One of Kelvin's hands slipped under her dress and into her panties. He rubbed her pearl, and a wave rippled through her body. She cried out as Kelvin's fingers caressed her folds at the same time his thumb played with her nub. Lara let out a few more cries before reaching under her dress. She tried to move his hand away but couldn't.

Her panties were wet.

"Kelvin…" The name came out between deep breaths.

He slid her panties down her legs and over her shoes. He held them up to his nose and inhaled before dropping them on the floor.

Embarrassment filled Lara, but he soon distracted her when he unbuttoned his shirt. Even in the darkness of the room, his massive chest and defined shoulders were evident. She didn't want to deny herself, so she reached behind her and turned on a soft, dimmed light by the bed.

Kelvin's pecs were smooth, round, and well defined. He had two prominent nipples, and his shoulders were two mounds of muscle. Biceps as thick as her thighs, leading to large, muscular forearms. He had washboard abs like a god out of classical mythology.

He lifted her dress and spread her legs, and his mouth explored her wet folds. She squealed and gripped the fabric of her comforter.

His tongue swabbed the liquid glaze that covered her channel. He pushed his face against her and his tongue probed deeper.

Lara's body rocked with the heat moving through her. His thumb teased her sweet bump again, and within moments, Lara cried out from an intense climax.

"I…" Lara could barely speak.

Kelvin took her in his arms and held her. Fascinated by

his ripped and cut physique, Lara ran her hand over his rock-hard pectoral muscles. She took one of his pronounced nipples between her thumb and forefinger, and it made his pec flex.

Hmmmm.

She leaned forward and took the other nipple in her mouth and gently sucked on it.

What am I doing?

Kelvin let out a deep groan and held her head in place.

Lara's tongue gently licked his nipple.

He moaned again, and she tugged on his other nipple.

"Lara, it's hot in here. Get out of that dress."

He stood up and removed his shoes, followed by his pants, revealing a large bulge in his underwear.

Lara sat up, kicked off her shoes, and slipped out of her dress. When she turned back around, he was completely nude. His phallus, thicker than anything she'd imagined, jutted straight out from his body and was already sheathed.

He reached out his hand and guided Lara back down on the bed. He placed his mouth over hers and she moaned. She wanted him, and his fierce kisses made her melt. She flung an arm around his back, and his strong body pressed against hers. His mouth moved back down to her throat, and she cried out his name.

He's hitting spots I didn't know I had.

With deliberate movements, his tongue licked her neck, and he nibbled on her earlobe. Moans emanated from her as he stimulated her tender flesh. His hands groped her breasts again, and his mouth devoured her nipples.

"Kelvin!"

Lara moaned as he sucked on her nipple. Moist and on the verge of exploding, she squirmed as he touched her sweet pearl and brought her to another climax.

How many is that?

Her body shivered, and her labored breath steadied. Flat on her back, she didn't want to move. Her body shook from the anticipation of what would happen next.

Kelvin parted her knees and placed his erection against her folds.

Paralyzed, she gazed up at him, trembling like a small girl standing in the snow waiting for the school bus.

He slid inside her.

"Ahh!" Lara cried sharply. "Kelvin!"

She threw her hands up to his chest. He paused for a moment. Lara took a few quick breaths, then grabbed his nipples and tugged. He thrust in all the way and she grabbed onto his massive triceps. They were even harder than his chest.

He must do a hundred push-ups a day to get triceps like that.

Why am I thinking about his triceps now?

Kelvin continued to thrust into her, and Lara cried out with each movement. He stretched her, and she wanted more. With every inch of him inside her, she moaned louder and louder.

BOOM! BOOM! BOOM! BOOM!

Lara froze, and Kelvin stopped his pumping motion.

"What was that?" he asked.

Lara was quiet for a moment. "It sounded like it was coming from downstairs."

"A neighbor?"

"A little old lady in a wheelchair. I think she hit something against her ceiling. Maybe a broom handle?"

"Should we stop?"

She squeezed his arms. "No."

Kelvin smiled and rammed deep inside her. Lara let out another sharp cry, and the *BOOM! BOOM! BOOM! BOOM!* continued. She didn't care. She encouraged him to keep going, and he did, pounding deep inside her. She screamed with just about every thrust of his hard cock. She was getting fucked tonight, and nothing would hold her back.

He rubbed her nub and sent her into yet another loud orgasm. The neighbor continued to bang on the ceiling, which caused them both to collapse into laughter.

"Hey...I have an idea," Lara said.

"What?"

"The sofa pulls out into a bed. Let's move this to the living room."

He hoisted her up into his arms and carried her into the living room. She removed the cushions from the sofa, and he opened up the bed for them. She kept it made up with clean sheets in case of unexpected guests. All she needed was a pillow or two, and she grabbed those from a closet.

Much to her amazement, Kelvin's erection never went down. With him fully hard and ready to go, she couldn't wait for more. She got on her back, grabbed her ankles, and welcomed him inside. He pushed deep into her, and she gripped his hard, muscular shoulders.

Lara wanted it to go on and on. As she finally let go, the ecstasy of good sex with a compatible man brought out a long-repressed passionate woman.

Kelvin made love to her all night.

Hours later, Lara's eyes fluttered open. She usually slept on her side, but when she awoke, she was on her back. She stared at the ceiling for a moment and allowed her eyes to adjust. The sun was probably up, but she had room-darkening shades, so the room remained quite dark. Curiously, the small lamp by the bed was still on. She never slept with the lights on.

How did we get back in the bedroom?

Kelvin, also on his back, breathed heavily. His massive chest heaved up and down with every breath. Unlike her, he did not have the covers over him. In the dim light, she could see his large manhood lying across his abdomen. Even flaccid, it was huge.

How many times did we make love?

Lara had lost count. Climax after climax had shaken her body, but curiously, she could not remember Kelvin having an orgasm. She reached over and touched his nipple, which made his cock move slightly. She rubbed her thumb gently over it, and his cock began to swell. She carefully moved close to his chest and placed her lips around his nipple. His cock stood straight up. She glanced at him but he was still asleep.

I want to touch it.

Lara reached out and wrapped her fingers around it gingerly, so as not to disturb him. It swelled in her hand.

Now that's big.

The girth impressed her. She guessed the length was above average, but the thickness was more like a diet soda can. Kelvin stirred, and Lara pulled her hand away. He didn't wake up, but she didn't want him to lose his erection. She put her mouth around his nipple again, and in a moment, he rolled over on top of her.

He thrust into her without a condom, and she began feeling the reverberation through her body. She moaned and soon reached climax without any stimulation of her pearl. His breathing intensified. He continued pumping inside her until he pulled out with a loud groan and collapsed on top of her. His body jerked as he climaxed all over her. Nestled in the nape of her neck, Kelvin kissed her throat and glided over to her lips.

He scooped her into his gigantic arms and held her to his chest. She loved the way his chest pressed against her cheek.

"Sleep well?"

She nodded. "How did we end up back in bed?"

"That couch isn't so comfortable. I carried you back in here after you fell asleep."

"Oh…"

His hand touched her hair. His big hand cupped her face.

"Did you sleep okay?" she asked.

"Yes," he said. "Not that we slept much."

Lara needed a shower. "Excuse me." She slipped out of bed, grabbed a robe, and headed for the bathroom.

What am I doing?

She washed away the remnants of sex. Her attraction to Kelvin both comforted and frightened her. He put her completely at ease whenever she spent time with him. He was kind, genuine, and attentive. Yet her desire for him could almost be described as animalistic. She craved him. His smell, his taste, and his touch were with her at all times it seemed.

So dangerous.

When she emerged from the bathroom, Kelvin was snoring. That would give her some time to prepare breakfast. She started a pot of coffee and figured the smell would eventually wake him up. Lara poked around the fridge and tried to come up with breakfast. Pancakes were always a safe bet. She made them the old-fashioned way with milk, eggs, and oil.

"Can I use your bathroom?" He stood before her naked. In the bright kitchen light she could see every cut of his defined physique. His dark chocolate skin glistened in the light. His cock wasn't fully erect but stood at attention nevertheless.

I took that all night long.

"Yes, of course." It was cute that he'd asked. With the sorry state her sweaty body had been in this morning, she imagined he needed a shower as well. She placed the wire whisk aside and turned on the gas range. Lara covered the skillet with shortening. She always burned her pancakes if she used oil or butter on the skillet. Hopefully, these would come out golden brown.

When she had a nice stack prepared, Lara set the table for breakfast. A few minutes later, Kelvin appeared, dressed.

"I need to grab something out of my car."

"Okay," Lara said.

He had a condom in his pocket last night.

Kelvin certainly came prepared. Lara wasn't sure if that was overconfidence or just a guy thing.

He returned with a backpack and went into the bathroom. She hoped Kelvin wasn't one of those people who liked his syrup heated up. Lara preferred it room temperature. She heated some up just in case.

"Smells good." He emerged from the bathroom in shorts and a T-shirt. "Good morning." He planted a kiss on her lips. His breath was fresh.

"Good morning. I hope you like pancakes."

"Love 'em. Who doesn't?"

He dug into the pancakes.

She was still awkward after a night of lovemaking, but she struggled to relax in his company.

He put down his coffee mug. "Do you have any plans today?"

"No, I don't make plans. Didn't we have that conversation yet?"

Kelvin laughed. "Yeah, I think we did. Your weeks are so busy you don't like the pressure of making plans on the weekends."

"You got it."

"You wanna go for a drive?"

Oh, gosh, what now?

Lara cocked her head. "Hmmm…"

"It'll be a fun way to spend the day."

After last night, how can I think about today?

"We can take a drive down to Bakersville. I can show you where I stay."

Lara gave in. "Sounds like a plan."

"There you go making plans…."

She threw her head back. She liked his playfulness. She hadn't expected their date to continue into the next day. Better to be with Kelvin in her own home than up against a door at Vista Terrace.

In his presence, she forgot about everything else. The stress of Miss Hawthorne's micromanaging, the suppressed pain of her adolescence, and her unwillingness to let go with a man. Until now.

After several wet kisses, they were driving down Route 165 in his car with the windows rolled down. The morning breeze blew through Lara's hair, and the relief of getting out of Portsmith washed through her.

Bakersville, part of the Niles Independent School District, took at least forty-five minutes to reach. Kelvin had quite a commute to Vista Terrace every day. Tall, green trees soared above the sides of the road. Lara spotted at least one deer in the woods. She couldn't imagine that long of a commute every day, no matter how beautiful.

"Take some deep breaths." He chuckled.

She followed his advice. Her nostrils filled with the scent of fresh pine. She closed her eyes, leaned back against the headrest, and let her sense of smell do the rest. Kelvin reached for her hand.

Lara's heart leapt as she recalled the previous night. She'd surrendered to Kelvin, and given herself to a man in a way she'd never dreamed possible. For the first time in her life, she'd enjoyed sex. Reclaimed it. Made it hers.

After a few more deep breaths, they'd pulled into an entranceway with a sign that read *private road*. The long, winding, two-lane blacktop led them deep into the country, away from the main route.

Bakersville resembled something out of a storybook. Colorful, bright flowers growing everywhere, clean air, and lush greenery. Kelvin guided Lara on a stroll through one of the most beautiful estates she'd ever seen. The rock paths and running brooks gave it the appearance of a state park or historical landmark. It turned out to be property owned by Kelvin's family.

The wealth of the Young family hadn't been exaggerated. They must own half the land in the town if this estate was any example.

"I have a crazy idea." Kelvin and Lara were strolling hand in hand through a breathtaking garden.

"I love crazy ideas…I think." Lara said. "Nothing crazier than last night?"

"Was last night crazy?" Kelvin squeezed her hand.

"No." Lara gazed around the vast estate. "Last night was amazing."

"Let's drive to Darrow."

"Darrow? I've never heard of Darrow. What's there?"

"You'll see," Kelvin teased. "I haven't been there for years. The last time I went was with my grandmother."

"Any hints?"

"No, it'll be a surprise."

Lara glanced at him with a questioning smirk. "I'm not sure I can handle another surprise."

The surprise between his legs had been enough for one weekend. Or one lifetime. The surprise of her taking it all night was something else altogether.

Within a short while, they were back on 165 heading south. Lara had no idea how far they were going, and she didn't really care. This weekend, an escape from the stress of Vista Terrace was exactly what she needed.

And the escape from sexual repression.

Kelvin had brought her into a new world. The passion he'd unleashed was a revelation. Lara hadn't known she had it in her to enjoy sex. Last night was the first time she'd ever made love due to her accord. Drowsy, she closed her eyes and drifted off to sleep.

Lara's eyes focused when she awoke.

Where am I?

Cool air brushed against her face. The windows were rolled up and the air conditioning turned on. She was in a car with a man she'd met a short time ago, going someplace she'd never been before. Her chest tightened and her heart raced.

"I kept you up too late last night." Kelvin's voice was soft.

She shook her head. He'd been the one who was *up* all night. She took a few deep breaths to help regulate her heart rate. "Was I asleep long?"

"Yes."

"Where did you say we were going?" Lara's gazed darted all over the place.

"Darrow."

"Is it far?" Her temples pulsed.

"Kinda sorta."

Lara didn't really like surprises, despite having given in. Why had she gone with this one? She could trust Kelvin. Couldn't she? Besides, hadn't he said he went there with his grandmother?

"Want some music?"

"Sure."

He turned on the car's radio. The drive seemed endless. She sighed—the time to ask questions was before they'd left, not now.

Somewhere he took his grandmother. How bad can it be?

The long drive, although it cleared her mind, also took its toll on Lara's backside. She really needed to get up and stretch.

"Can you stop at the next available restroom?"

He nodded.

She was grateful when he finally pulled over. The general store looked like any other along the road of a small town. She found the restroom and glanced at her watch. They had driven for hours.

When Lara finished, she strolled around the store and picked up two bottles of cold water. Her stomach rumbled, but she decided to ignore food for now. She wasn't sure what Kelvin had in mind. In fact, she was clueless since he hadn't told her anything. At the register, she glanced outside. He still sat in the car. Either he'd taken a very quick leak or his bladder was as strong as the rest of him.

She returned to the car and handed Kelvin a bottle of water.

"Thank you. We're almost there."

"Almost where?"

"Houmas House."

"And what's that?"

"An old Louisiana plantation. I think some of my ancestors may have worked there." Kelvin grinned.

She didn't. In fact, that statement made her uncomfortable.

Why is he taking me there?

In a few minutes, the sign for Houmas House came into view, and he turned into the drive. It was a stately manor with bright white columns, and it also looked strangely familiar. Lara didn't believe in déjà vu, but she had an odd feeling she'd been here before. Yet that wasn't possible.

"Kelvin, this place looks awfully familiar."

It came to her. Chills went through her body. Houmas House was the location of the horror film *Hush… Hush, Sweet Charlotte*.

CHAPTER TEN

Lara blinked. She couldn't believe what she was seeing. "Oh, my, yes. That's it. Kelvin, why are we here?"

"Afternoon tea."

We drove hours for afternoon tea?

"There's a restaurant here?"

"More than one."

"Wow. I've never been to afternoon tea before." What she meant was no man had ever taken her to tea before. At least, not on a date. She'd been to high tea when she visited London during a semester.

Lara stepped out of the car and gazed at the grand manor. A majestic two-story structure, it boasted slender columns and an upstairs balcony. She hadn't seen the film in years, but it was one of her favorites. She always tried to catch it when it was broadcast on one of the classic movie channels.

Kelvin led her by the arm inside. Once they were seated, they were greeted with a glass of champagne.

He raised his glass. "To sleepless nights."

She laughed. "Can I rephrase that?"

"Please do."

"Hmmm…how about to waking up with you?" But how much longer could it go on? How much longer could temptation last? Was the risk worth jeopardizing years of hard work and college tuition?

He touched her glass with his. "Good call."

A server placed a platter of various sandwiches on their table. "Which tea will you be enjoying today, ma'am?" Lara and Kelvin looked over the tea list and placed their order.

Lara's stomach still grumbled, so she wasted no time grabbing a sandwich. Turkey and watercress with Creole mayonnaise, it was delicious and just what she needed. Kelvin had class.

"How is it?" he asked. His silky almond eyes shimmered in the afternoon light.

"They're nice. And I'm not saying that just because I'm hungry."

Hungry for more of you.

Lara reached for an open-faced Cajun caviar with crème fraiche. "I can see why your grandmother likes this place."

"It's not just the food. She's a huge Bette Davis fan." Kelvin bit into his sandwich, and she watched the rhythmic motion of his large lips that had kissed her all night. The lips that had caressed her body from head to toe. How could one man be so passionate?

"What's that one?"

"Brie with kumquat chutney."

Lara eyed another one on the plate. "I love Brie. But I thought tea always included cucumber sandwiches?"

"It does." Kelvin pointed to the middle of the tray. "The ones on the white bread are cucumber with garden herb spread."

Spread. She'd spread her legs for him and ached for more. And he'd given her more until she fell asleep exhausted and sated.

Lara took a sip of her tea. It was Earl Grey and it complemented the sandwiches brilliantly. She gazed around the room filled with lattice and wicker chairs. Bringing her here was a highly romantic gesture on Kelvin's part. But was she ready for romance?

After last night, she should be ready for anything. She'd crossed that threshold and had to experience all the postcoital emotions that came along with it. Guilt. Euphoria. Shame. Satisfaction. Embarrassment. Joy. They swirled through her mind although fleetingly.

"The best's yet to come." That twinkle in his eye could mean he had more lovemaking in store for her tonight.

Lara gazed at Kelvin, her mouth dry and cheeks burning. "What do you mean?"

"You haven't sampled the canapé course." The deep bass in his voice added richness to his words.

Lara bit into the briny Brie. "Bring it on."

Within minutes, the server presented an array of canapés. Lara feasted on duck confit salad with pickled quail eggs and smoked salmon-wrapped asparagus. Kelvin selected the poached shrimp and chicken salad. By the time the scones course came, they were both stuffed.

They joined one of the tours to walk off their feast, and Lara marveled at the history represented. She hadn't ventured out on excursions to learn about her state's past since she'd been in school.

"This is an incredible place." Lara's neck stretched back as she stared at the intricate woodwork.

"My grandmother felt a special connection to this place. It wasn't just the nostalgia of being a movie buff."

"What kind of connection?"

"She never put it into words, but I believe it had something to do with a grandparent. Or great-grandparent. She was intentionally vague. It always upset my mother when she spoke about it, so she seldom did."

"Why did it upset your mother?"

"She's never said." Kelvin shrugged.

It didn't seem right to probe any further. Lara kept her focus on the architecture for the rest of the tour.

Within an hour, they were back on the road.

"I didn't mean to kidnap you," Kelvin said, his voice laced with playfulness.

"That was awfully far, considering I slept through a part of the drive."

"You weren't asleep as long as you thought." He reached for her hand.

The gesture relaxed her, not that she was uneasy. The touch of his hand made her melt into the car seat.

"Thank you, Kelvin. That was a special treat."

"My pleasure."

Afternoon tea intended to be small bites to stave off hunger until the main meal. Was this an Americanized version, or would she get hungry later?

The drive was long but pleasant. Lara savored the variety of flavors still lingering on her palette, and she admired Kelvin for choosing something so unique. They stopped once for a restroom break, and this time Kelvin did indeed use the facilities.

She'd gotten a text from Cassie and sent a quick reply. *Will catch up with you later.* The events of this weekend were certainly one for the history books.

When they reached Bakersville, they stopped for a second time. Kelvin decided a light meal was in order, so he treated Lara to dinner—a salad, as that was all she could handle.

"I had an amazing time today," Lara said.

"I did, too. I've kept you away from home far too long. I'd better get you back."

The evening wasn't over.

It was dark when they arrived at Lara's condo, and she was grateful to be home. Her little place wasn't much, but it was comfortable.

"May I take a shower?" Kelvin asked.

"Of course." She still found it so cute that he asked. While he was in the bathroom, Lara opened a bottle of chilled white wine. She poured herself a glass and savored the cool flavor.

A shower's a good idea.

She would take one as soon as Kelvin was finished. It was a long day. Most of it was spent in the car, but Lara was still tired. He might still be hungry but she decided against cheese. She sliced up some apples and placed them on a tray with his glass of wine.

Lara turned on the television to entertain Kelvin when it was her turn in the shower. She left the remote by the tray and sat on the couch to enjoy her wine while waiting for him to come out of the bathroom.

"My turn," Lara said when Kelvin emerged, a large towel wrapped around his waist. His muscles glistened with droplets of water. She couldn't wait to shower, or rather, couldn't wait to be freshly clean and ready for Kelvin.

The mirror was still completely fogged over. The bathroom was more like a steam room, but Lara didn't care. She turned on the water and stepped into the nice, hot streams.

When she was finished, Kelvin sat on the couch, towel still draped around his waist, as she headed to the bedroom. She lit come candles and put on some music. When the room was ready, she turned to find him standing in the doorway. The towel fell from his waist and landed on the floor, his cock hard and ready. He stepped into the room and took her into his arms.

She pressed her lips against his and her tongue meshed with his. She wanted him even more tonight than she had last night. The ache deep within her core signaled her longing for him. Waves of heat surged and her breasts swelled.

Kelvin eased her gently onto the bed, and she ran her hands over his strong back muscles. She still wore her bathrobe yet his dick swelled against her.

His tongue probed her mouth. Lara grabbed onto his strong shoulders, pulling him to her. She clasped her hands around his neck as though she didn't want him to move. The heat raged within her.

He slipped on a condom and pulled her robe open and then got on top of her and entered her slowly. She cried out from the thickness of his massive dick and took a few deep breaths. Once again, Kelvin made love to her all night.

**

In the quiet of the predawn hour, Lara lay on her back gazing at the ceiling. Her vision had long ago adjusted to the darkness of the room. She'd drifted off to sleep after hours of lovemaking, but now awake, she reflected on how far she'd come.

The steady rhythm of Kelvin's breathing soothed her and conveyed peacefulness. Being in the same bed with a man both aroused and frightened her, but not in a dangerous way. The fear was related to how addictive he'd become.

No longer shackled by the damage done to her as a girl, she'd embraced the affection of a man who'd unleashed her long-dormant passion.

But would it last?

Desire was a fleeting emotion. She'd been caught up in Kelvin's allure, his magnetism, and his unyielding sexual prowess in bed. Sailing on the waves of passion, she didn't kid herself that she could come down from this high as easily as she'd given into it.

Feeling as if it were floating on the mattress, her body had never been so sated in her life. The endorphin rush left her euphoric yet in a state of total relaxation at the same time.

But it was wrong. She stood directly above him in the chain of command at work. She jeopardized his position and hers if anyone knew. And someone did know.

CHAPTER ELEVEN

After breakfast, and many kisses, Kelvin drove away from Lara's place. He'd never been with a woman whom he didn't want to leave. He had to force himself to hit the road.

He had plenty of things to do to prepare for the workday tomorrow, and he was certain Lara did as well. He'd taken up enough of her time.

But what a great time.

Lara had depth. She was stable, confident, and independent. He admired how far she had made it in a relatively short time. Only twenty-seven and already a vice-principal, she'd made some truly impressive accomplishments in her career.

I want to be with her.

His grip tightened on the steering wheel as he relished memories of her slick heat. He'd lost count of how many times he'd thrust inside her, and how his body had shaken from the intensity of the sex.

More than sex.

Trustworthy—a quality he respected yet hadn't found often in a woman. He also admired Lara's ambition. She had goals and strived to make herself better.

And she keeps up with me in bed.

He managed to tire most women out after a short time. Lara seemed to hunger for him, as though she hadn't had a man in a while. Or perhaps just not the right man. It was a blessing to find a woman like Lara.

The drive back to Bakersville relaxed him. He'd met a woman worth pursuing. The sweetness of her kisses and the fullness of her breasts filled his mind on the rest of the way home. More than once, he had to mop his brow over the shiver that shook his body, betraying his want and need for Lara.

He'd need a nap soon. He had some things he needed to prepare for this week's lessons but didn't have all the resources he needed. And he'd forgotten to tell Lara he would need to bother her again to take him to the dreaded book room.

When he reached home, Kelvin sent Lara a text: *Need to access book room tomorrow.* Lara sent back a text: *Meet me there during your planning time.* That settled, he could catch some sleep and then get to work.

**

Since five thirty in the morning, his usual workout time, Kelvin had moved his arms together, and the weights had slid up the pole. His huge pectorals swelled with each inward movement and relaxed when he opened his arms. His chest regime relaxed him. He did this exercise sitting down and it gave him time to think.

There's a strange vibe at that school.

Kelvin loved his career. He'd been rewarded as a teacher and recognized as a strong coach. He was blessed in the sense that he got up every morning looking forward to going to work. He went to bed each night looking forward to the next day. Vista Terrace was different. There were some mornings he pulled up in his car with an awkward feeling at the bottom of his stomach.

This too shall pass.

It was still the beginning of the year. This was only his second school district. He'd spent his eight previous years teaching in the same place.

Perhaps it's the change.

No. What had happened over the past week or so was not just change. He and Lara were clearly being targeted. They weren't imagining it. Kelvin always kept a positive attitude, so he'd get through it.

He set the weights down and headed for the locker room. Kelvin was ready to face the day and make it a good one. He stripped down and tossed his clothes into his locker, then stepped into the shower. The hot water pelted against his pumped chest as he lathered up his muscular body.

Kelvin finished, dried off, and headed for the mirrors to apply some deodorant and brush his teeth. He planned on having a good year at Vista Terrace despite all odds. Back at his locker, he pulled a shirt over his head, and his freshly pumped pecs nearly stressed the seams.

The air was crisp on the morning drive up to Vista Terrace. The tree-lined country road and the long drive gave him time to think each day. He looked forward to football practice after school, seeing his team be the best they could be.

The first game of the year, only a few weeks away, was already the talk of Vista Terrace. His team would face off against their main rival, Linford Middle School.

Kelvin arrived on campus early. He liked having time to himself in his classroom, to double-check that everything was set up for the day and take care of anything he might have missed. He didn't like feeling rushed. He couldn't understand the teachers who rolled up five minutes before the bell rang. There were several of them here who did that.

"Morning, Mr. Young." Lewis's furrowed brow betrayed an uneasiness. It almost appeared as though he wasn't merely greeting Kelvin, but wanted to speak with him.

"Good morning, Lewis." Kelvin greeted him with a broad smile and continued walking. Usually, Kelvin enjoyed being outgoing and friendly. He liked to connect with people. At this school, he'd discovered even small talk could be a mistake.

He strolled down his corridor. Strode's light was on and the door open, but Strode was apparently not in the room.

What the hell does he do?

Vista Terrace had no shortage of oddballs, but Kelvin was grateful for someone as stable as Lara. She kept him grounded. She had a calm spirit, which he found comforting. And she managed to avoid drama and seemed content. Unlike most women, she had asked nothing of him. Their time together made Kelvin feel like he'd found an equal.

"How are you doing today, Mr. Young?"

Did Lewis follow me here?

"I'm doing fine, Lewis. Yourself?"

"Doin' just fine myself. You seen Mr. Strode?" Lewis didn't make direct eye contact and shifted nervously from one foot to the other.

"No, I haven't."

"I was just wondering why he keeps the lights on when he's not in the room. Waste of electricity, you know?"

"Good luck finding him." Kelvin turned his attention back to his work, and Lewis disappeared out of view.

This school's full of nosy people.

Kelvin didn't want to get involved with that. He preferred to keep his distance from gossip and avoid the pettiness at Vista Terrace—see his young boys and girls grow into responsible young adults. His mission focused on his students and their achievements.

And on Lara.

He longed for his arms to be wrapped around her soft, sweet body. But they couldn't do that at work.

Something caught his attention. It was a sound coming from the hallway. Strode breeze by his doorway, followed by the sound of another door closing. It must have been the door to Strode's classroom.

Weird.

Stealthy movements seemed to be the norm in this school. Kelvin decided to ignore it and focus on his job. His students were more important than getting worked up about the backstabbing at Vista Terrace.

"Good morning." The librarian stood in the doorway. "I have those books you requested ready for you in the library, Mr. Strode."

"It's Mr. Young, and that's the second time you've done that."

"Oh, really? An honest mistake."

"Is it? Thanks for your trouble." He turned away from her.

"I'm sorry," she said followed by the clickity-clack of her heels against the freshly buffed floor. Two black guys on campus who looked nothing alike got mistaken for each other.

Or do we?

Kelvin had no idea if anyone called Strode "Mr. Young" because Strode was too antisocial to speak to anyone. Curious, Kelvin got out of his chair and stepped into the hallway. Strode was not in his room.

But hadn't he just gone in there?

Kelvin couldn't be sure. Had Strode entered his classroom? Had the door shut quietly?

"Good morning, Mr. Young."

He hoped the surprise didn't register on his face. Miss Hawthorne always summoned teachers to her office. It was rare for her to approach a teacher.

"Good morning, Miss Hawthorne. How are you today?" He turned back toward his room. The last thing he needed was Hawthorne seeing him snoop, just like everyone else.

"I'm well, thank you. You did a good job during Dr. Hamilton's visit. I want to commend you for that."

Not "I commend you" but "I want to."

"Thank you, Miss Hawthorne."

"I think some of our new teachers could benefit from observing you. I may set up some times for them to come in and watch you work if you don't mind."

"That will be fine, ma'am."

"Have a good day."

"You too, ma'am."

Kelvin's eyes stayed focused on the doorway after Miss Hawthorne went away. He tried to process what she'd said. Sure, it was a compliment. He appreciated that.

But a compliment at what cost?

Within a few minutes, the bell rang, and students started filing into Kelvin's room. His mood brightened. The students always reminded him of the real reason he was here.

An aide arrived from the library with the books he'd requested. Now all he had to do was go to the book room during his planning period, and he would have the materials he needed for the week.

Hours later, when his break finally rolled around, he headed for the book room. The door was ajar and a light was on. Kelvin carefully closed the door behind him. He peered down several aisles before he found Lara.

"Hey, good afternoon."

Lara forced a weak smile, her face filled with furrows of stress.

"Glad it's been good for you. This has been one of those Mondays."

"How bad is it?" Kelvin glided the back of his hand along her cheek.

After an intake of breath, Lara closed her eyes and brushed her lips across his flesh.

He took her into his arms and kissed her, wanting to rub some of the stress out of her day. Her body was tense and she needed to relax.

"Kelvin, this isn't the place."

"I know, baby, I know. I just want to make you feel better."

He kissed her again, and she responded. He led her down to the floor littered with papers and fallen books.

"Kelvin, not here."

"You need to release that tension."

He continued to kiss her while slipping one hand under her skirt. Even though he had just made love to her Saturday night, he already missed her taste. He pushed his tongue into her mouth and rubbed her bead. She squirmed underneath him, and he slid two fingers into her folds.

"Kelvin…."

He had to finish what he started and slid her panties down.

She grabbed his wrist. "Kelvin…"

When she said his name, it didn't sound like a protest.

He kissed her deeply, then moved his head down between her legs. His tongue played with her pearl while his fingers explored inside her. She writhed and moaned, and he went for the release that she needed. Her body shuddered but he didn't stop. He kept going until he brought her to a second climax.

Good thing I locked the door.

There really wasn't much traffic outside the T buildings. It was unlikely anyone wandered by.

Lara sat up. "Didn't you need some books?"

"Yes." Kelvin helped her up off the floor. "Some student workbooks. Eighth grade science."

"Well, let's find some. Your break is almost over."

Kelvin returned to his room, a stack of workbooks in his arms, just in time for his next class. But he could barely concentrate on anything academic. His legs weak and heart still racing, he sat at his desk and tried to regulate his breathing.

Panic stabbed through him. Lara had been right all along—their attraction to one another was dangerous. Doing something so foolish at work could only lead to trouble. He took a few sips from his water bottle as the last few kids filed into his classroom.

The rest of the day went relatively well. During the last class of the day, the counselor appeared at his door.

"Miss Hawthorne needs to see you. I'll hold your class 'til you get back."

Kelvin frowned. It was not at all unusual for Miss Hawthorne to expect teachers to stop teaching if she wanted to see them here and now. He found it annoying if not disrespectful.

"Yes, ma'am." He smiled at the counselor and headed to the office.

When he got there, the secretary reached for her intercom and buzzed Miss Hawthorne. "Mr. Young is here."

At least she got my name right.

The door to Miss Hawthorne's office opened and she ushered him in. She closed the door behind him and gestured for him to take a seat.

"This is Prudence Hall, Director of Certified Personnel."

Kelvin nodded and shook her hand.

"And this is Leona Page, Director of School Performance"

Miss Page pressed her lips together, and Miss Hawthorne took a seat.

Prudence Hall immediately turned to Kelvin. "Mr. Young, a sixth grade girl said that you took her into a custodian's closet and molested her."

CHAPTER TWELVE

A wave of nausea ran through Kelvin's stomach and permeated his body. A faint ringing in his ears started low and then increased.

"She's not a student whom you teach," Miss Hall said.

"She's not even in the same wing of the building you teach in." Miss Page sat stoically on the opposite side of the table.

Kelvin's body froze. His mouth went dry, and he couldn't speak if he wanted to.

"There's a procedure we have to follow and it involves an investigation. In order to expedite this, we are placing you on administrative leave. You will still be paid. Think of it as working from home." Hall handed him a letter.

The letter said essentially what she had just stated, plus added a part that forbade Kelvin to set foot on any Portsmith Independent School District property until further notice.

"You'll be contacted by our internal investigator," Hall said.

"And we've done our own investigation," Miss Hawthorne said cheerfully.

Somehow, Kelvin got the impression her words were supposed to be comforting.

"Sometimes kids will say anything, Mr. Young," Miss Page said.

"I've been accused of all kinds of things." Miss Hawthorne shrugged.

Again, Kelvin got the feeling she was trying to relax him.

"We have to let the investigation run its course," Page said.

"How long will that take?" Kelvin spoke in a soft, even voice. He could barely get the words out.

"We don't know, Mr. Young. It could take days or it could take weeks." Miss Hall was not smiling.

"What do I do until then?" His cheeks burned.

"Do nothing," Miss Hall said sharply. "And speak to no one. This is a private matter, which hopefully will not go public. The only way it will is if the parent decides to cause trouble."

"Some parents think their problems can be solved on the six-o'clock news," Page said with a slight chuckle. "The child didn't make the complaint at the school. She called the parent, and the parent called me. That's why I'm here."

"If you've done nothing wrong, you have nothing to worry about." Miss Hawthorne spoke to Kelvin with assurance. It was the second time today that she'd spoken with sincerity, the first when he'd seen her in the hallway early this morning.

"But how will my absence be explained?"

"It won't," Hall said curtly. "You're absent. Nothing more, nothing less."

"Discretion is key here." Miss Page nodded.

"It won't go outside this room, Mr. Young," Miss Hawthorne said. "If anyone asks where you are, you're absent."

"Speak to no one about this," Miss Hall repeated. "Miss Hawthorne will escort you to your room. You can collect your personal items." Miss Hall spoke in a monotone, almost as though her lines were rehearsed. "Then Miss Hawthorne will escort you to your car. You will leave campus immediately."

Miss Hawthorne looked at the clock. "It's only nine minutes before the bell rings. Can't Mr. Young dismiss his class for the day?"

"No," Hall answered, her voice frosty.

Hawthorne tilted her head and paused. "Okay, Mr. Young, let's go."

Miss Hawthorne walked him out of the office. The others remained behind.

"I'm in shock," Kelvin whispered.

"I'm in shock, too," she said. After they walked a few more steps, she stopped. "Mr. Young, I'm not going to escort you to your car. Go to your room, gather your things, and Miss Logan will dismiss your class."

He nodded and continued down the corridor. His feet were like lead. The ringing in his ears continued, yet his heartbeat remained oddly normal.

"Is everything okay, Mr. Young?" The voice vaguely registered as one of his student's, but he couldn't answer. He really was in shock. He methodically picked up his teacher's bag and left the room. Miss Logan gazed at him with a peculiar expression.

He walked directly to his car. He started the engine, but his hands were shaking. He drove carefully off the lot and headed home. His mind raced. His career could be ruined. If it went public, it would destroy his family's good name. Lara might not believe him and might never want to see him again.

This is insane, but it'll blow over in a few days.

He might miss a few days of practice with his team but they could catch up. Kelvin's hands were shaking on the steering wheel. There was a possibility it wouldn't blow over in a few days. How many times had he seen a teacher's picture in the paper or on the news? This was one of those things that happened to other people, not to Kelvin Young.

The panic that had seized him earlier was now tenfold. He could barely concentrate on the traffic in front of him. Everything blurred, and he couldn't focus.

Will Lara believe me?

They'd said it would not go outside the room. That was bull. From the look on the counselor's face, he suspected she'd already been briefed.

Does that mean it'll be all over the school tomorrow?

He couldn't worry about that right now. He'd basically been sent home to let the investigation run its course. Tortured as to whether or not he should call Lara, he reminded himself that he had to follow protocol. Miss Page had spoken about discretion, but he could tell Lara, couldn't he? She needed her to hear it from him first.

**

Lara vomited into the ladies' room wastebasket for the third time. The school cafeteria lunch she'd eaten today came up with a vengeance. She'd even vomited onto her dress.

Miss Logan handed her some bottled water.

"I don't need any damn water."

Logan placed the bottle on the counter. "Please, Lara, try to calm down. Someone might hear you."

Lara? I'm not on a first-name basis with her.

"Your throat's going to be parched from throwing up. The water will help soothe it."

"I need something hot, like tea." As soon as she said the word *tea*, she retched into the wastebasket again. Miss Logan left the room, and Lara burst into tears. She'd finally met a man she'd thought she could trust. She'd given herself to Kelvin in a way she had never let go with any man before. And now look what he'd done.

Lara heaved into the basket again. Nothing came up except the memories of what Luke had done to her. He'd come into her room at night and done things to her, all the while pretending it was some sort of game. Her throat was on fire. Her eyes burned and the tears did nothing to cool them.

Her hands trembled as she tried to steady herself. With a heart that had dropped to her shoes, she pushed the wastebasket away, hoping to push the memories away with it.

They remained, seared into her mind like a recurring nightmare.

She lifted herself up off the floor and looked in the mirror. A pathetic-looking mess stared back at her. Rumpled hair, stained dress, streaked makeup, and her eyes were red. Blood vessels had burst from the retching.

Tears continued to run down her face, and her body couldn't stop shaking. Her legs were weak. She grabbed the bottle of water, unscrewed the cap, and took a drink. It did help—but just a little. She tried to rub the mess off her dress, but it was useless. All the children would be gone by now. There were no extra-curricular activities on Mondays, but there were plenty of adults on campus who would see her.

No, they're all in a faculty meeting.

Now was her chance to get away. She could care less what Miss Hawthorne thought of her skipping the meeting. But since no Hawthorne messenger had arrived summoning her, Logan must have passed the word along that Lara was sick. No, ill. Kelvin was the one who was sick.

She stepped outside the ladies' room. There was no one in sight. She hurried to her office to get her bag. Sitting on her desk was a steaming hot cup of tea. She sat in her chair and stared at it for a moment.

When did Miss Logan develop a heart?

Lara scolded herself for being callous. She'd never taken the opportunity to get to know Miss Logan. The woman had just been someone who sat in on meetings. It appeared as though she sympathized with Lara.

But why?

She put the cup up to her lips. The tea burned her throat, but she didn't care. That pain was almost an escape. After draining the liquid, she put the cup down and rushed off as quietly as she could.

The drive home became a blur. The tears wouldn't stop. Her knuckles blanched from gripping the steering wheel too hard, but somehow, she managed to get home in one piece.

When she dragged herself into her condo, she gazed around as though looking at it for the first time. Today, it was as though she looked at her life for the first time. So naïve. Too trusting.

Thankfully, she had cleaned up yesterday, so there were no remnants of *him* in her apartment. She'd barely put her bag down when the phone rang. She removed the phone from her purse. The call was from Kelvin. She flung the phone as hard as she could against the wall, and it shattered into several pieces.

She peeled her soiled clothing off and crawled into bed. She couldn't think about food, and she didn't even want a shower. Her head pounded, telling her she needed sleep as an escape. The sleep did not come easy. She tossed and turned until she lay still from mere exhaustion.

How can I face another day at Vista Terrace?

CHAPTER THIRTEEN

The next morning, Kelvin sat on his couch, numb. A coffee cup sat on the table, untouched. All he could think about were his students, filing into a classroom, and not being there to greet them. He couldn't go to work. In fact, he wasn't even sure he could call the school.

Administrative leave.

A sterile term to mask something ugly. He'd been told to do nothing. Never before had he been so helpless. The accusation had come out of nowhere and knocked him over like a bowling ball hitting a pin.

As he gazed at nothing in particular in the quiet of his living room, he reminded himself he should be cleared in no time. After all, he hadn't done anything. How could they keep him from doing his job?

He started a load of laundry as a way to occupy his time because he had no idea what else to do. It took an effort to push himself off the couch and put one foot in front of the other.

What a day.

A short time later, a knock at the door got his attention. Kelvin didn't have to ask who was there. He opened the door, smiled as best he could, and extended his hand.

"I'm Kelvin Young."

The gentleman on his porch was well dressed. He wore neatly pressed slacks, a knit shirt, and a fine leather jacket. With his left hand, he braced himself against the railing of Kelvin's porch. His right hand was against the left side of his body, hidden by his jacket. Kelvin assumed his hand rested on a gun.

After a beat, the man gripped Kelvin's hand. "I'm Detective Darryl Washington. Portsmith Police Department."

Kelvin looked directly into his eyes and—somehow—trusted him. "Please come in." Kelvin stepped back into the house and led the detective into the living room. He'd seen enough television to know he had better sit down first, so he did. The detective sat across from him.

"I'm here because of a complaint that allegedly took place at the Vista Terrace Middle School in Portsmith, Louisiana." The detective pulled a folder out of the bag that was slung over his shoulder. He opened the folder from the wrong side, and the paper spilled to the floor. Kelvin didn't bend over to help him pick them up. Making any kind of moves around an armed officer wasn't wise.

When the detective gathered up his papers, he began reading from one of them as though reading from a script. "You have the right to remain silent. Anything you say can and will be used against you in a court of law."

Kelvin wanted to make sure he was hearing the detective correctly.

"Excuse me," Kelvin said. "Am I being arrested?"

"No." Detective Washington shook his head. "Everyone I read this to thinks I'm arresting them. The Miranda Rights have to be read in order to question someone."

Kelvin nodded.

The detective looked down at his script and began reading again. "You have the right to remain silent. Anything you say can and will be used against you in a court of law. You have the right to have an attorney present during questioning. If you cannot afford an attorney, one will be appointed to you by a court of law. Do you understand your rights as I have read them to you?"

"Yes."

"Would you like an attorney present?"

"No." Kelvin's family would go ballistic if they found out he was questioned without an attorney, but he didn't care. He had nothing to hide and wanted this misunderstanding over with as soon as possible.

"Would you sign here please? You are indicating that I have read your rights to you and that you waive your right to an attorney."

Kelvin looked at the paper that Detective Washington put in front of him. Across the top of the page, in bold letters, it said YOU ARE UNDER ARREST / INVESTIGATION.

"I'm not signing anything that says I'm under arrest."

"Okay." The detective took the paper back, crossed out the word *arrest* and circled the word *investigation*. He handed it back to Kelvin.

Kelvin signed and dated the paper.

"The complaint, sir, is from a sixth grade girl." The detective glanced down at his paperwork. "Brandy Cartwright. Apparently she was in Miss Teal's class at the time of the incident and had asked to use the rest room. Are you familiar with that teacher?"

"No, I just started working at Vista Terrace this school year."

"I haven't been up to the school yet. I'll be going up there next to have a look at the layout of the school. See where Miss Teal's class is in relation to yours." Detective Washington shifted in his seat. "If the allegation turns out to be true, you are looking at a great deal of time. You can potentially mitigate that time by confessing. Did you do it?"

Kelvin looked him in the eyes and said, "No."

"Do you know a student named Brandy Cartwright?"

"No," Kelvin said. The last name, yes, but no one named Brandy.

"She specifically said your name."

Kelvin didn't know how to respond so he just shrugged. Detective Washington continued to question him for another twenty minutes or so. He asked him some of the same questions two or three times, presumably to see if Kelvin remained consistent. When he finished, Detective Washington stood up to leave.

"I'm sorry we had to meet under unfortunate circumstances," the detective said as he handed Kevin a business card. "I'll be in touch if I have any more questions."

Kelvin closed the door. In some odd way, he was relieved. That part was over. He'd known he would be interviewed by law enforcement. Getting that behind him put him one step closer to getting this nightmare over with.

Or did it?

Kelvin glanced at the business card in his hand. A name was crossed off, and Detective Washington's name was hand-written in ink. It wasn't even his own card.

Can this day get any stranger?

He attempted to call Lara several times—without getting any response.

A buzzing sound came from the laundry room. At least he had something to do to keep his mind off all this, if even for a moment. But as Kelvin pulled his laundry from the washing machine and loaded it into the dryer, he couldn't take his mind off of it. And maybe he shouldn't. This was serious.

He never showed me his badge.

Kelvin stood still, arms full of wet clothing.

He never showed me his badge, and I didn't ask.

Kelvin slowly dumped the rest of his clothes into the dryer. The man had introduced himself as a Portsmith police officer but showed no identification. Something smelled.

Am I being set up?

CHAPTER FOURTEEN

Lara lay in bed with the covers wrapped around her. She'd called in sick because she couldn't face the day. Her plan was to stay in bed all day, sleep, and try to forget. Nature didn't agree with that, and she crawled out of bed to use the bathroom. Not wanting to see what the ravages of little sleep and a lot of stress did to her, she avoided looking at herself in the mirror.

Her temples throbbed, and she gobbled down a few pills. The water refreshed her, and she downed the whole glass. Tap water had never tasted so good.

It wasn't every day her whole world came crashing down. That sick, empty feeling made her stomach ache, and no pill could make that go away. Only time.

Now that she was on her feet, she wandered into the living room with heaviness in her heart. Her feet, which she could barely lift, shuffled along the carpet. The remnants of her mobile phone lay shattered on the floor, as destroyed as her trust in men.

As broken as her alliance with Kelvin.

As crumbled as her life had become since yesterday.

Lara lumbered back to bed, her body and her mind racked with torment. But the pain in her soul hurt most. After what Luke had done to her during her adolescence, she hadn't been able to trust anyone. Yet she'd let her guard down with one man and look what happened.

How could I have allowed myself to trust Kelvin?

She wanted to reach out to someone and vent. Perhaps call Cassie. But at the moment, she didn't even have the energy. Oh, and she didn't have a phone.

She woke the following morning knowing she couldn't avoid Vista Terrace forever. It ached to get out of bed. That queasy feeling in her stomach hadn't gone away, and she dreaded setting foot on that campus again.

Lara showered and prepared for work but moved slowly. Her heart wasn't in it today, as she'd be subjected to stares and gossip. The counselor. The custodians. Probably everyone.

The emptiness hurt most of all. The hole in her heart, the feeling of shame and humiliation, and an overall helplessness.

When Lara arrived on campus, she checked in with Miss Hawthorne.

"Good morning, Miss Hawthorne."

"Good morning, Ms. Rumson. How are you feeling today?"

"Better, thank you. I was ill yesterday."

"Yes, Miss Logan told me. I'm glad you're here with us today."

Lara decided it would be a good idea to thank Miss Logan

for helping her on Monday. She never really had much contact with Logan. Lara found her office and knocked.

"Come in."

Logan sat behind her desk, staring at her computer.

"Good morning."

"Oh, good morning. I'm glad you're back."

Lara sat down across from her. "I wanted to thank you for your help on Monday."

"No problem."

"I was in terrible shape."

"Understandable."

"Is there any word on Mr. Young? I mean… the investigation?"

"Not that I know of. He sure has some explaining to do."

"How so?" Lara asked.

Miss Logan finally looked away from her computer. "He went missing the entire fourth period on Monday. No one saw him on his break. We were all questioned. Everyone on campus was questioned."

Lara's heart raced. Beads of sweat formed on her brow, and her mouth went dry.

"What about fourth period? Why is that important?"

"That's when the girl said it happened."

Lara's stomach began to rumble. She hadn't eaten anything today because she wasn't hungry.

I was with Kelvin fourth period in the book room.

Lara stood up. "I have a lot of work to catch up on. Thank you again."

"You're welcome." Logan returned to staring at her computer screen.

Lara hurried out of Logan's office.

Kelvin was with me.

Lara reached into her purse for her phone. She had to call Kelvin immediately to find out whom he'd told so far. He couldn't have done anything during fourth period. Lara's hand flailed about her bag until she remembered she didn't have a phone anymore.

Damn!

She went to her office and picked up the phone but hesitated before she dialed. She wasn't sure what the policy was regarding contacting a teacher on administrative leave.

"Ms. Rumson." It was Miss Hawthorne, standing in the doorway with a young lady. "Am I disturbing you?"

Lara put the phone down. "No, ma'am."

"Good. This is Miss Day. She'll be substitute teaching for Mr. Young's classes until he returns. We couldn't find anyone for yesterday, so we took turns holding his class."

Miss Hawthorne couldn't possibly be including herself.

"Please show Miss Day to Mr. Young's room. I'm sure you know where everything is, so you can help her get set up."

"Yes, ma'am."

Why is she sure I know where everything is?

"Come with me, Miss Day."

What does Hawthorne know?

CHAPTER FIFTEEN

Kelvin had been troubled all morning. After speaking with the detective yesterday, the serious nature of the charge kept sinking in deeper. He had to speak to someone. But speak to whom?

That lady…what was her name? Her job involved advocacy for teachers. Kelvin grabbed the tote bag he'd been given that day. The information had to be in there somewhere.

He recalled getting something about an organization. He flipped through paper after paper until he found it. A flyer for the North Louisiana Teachers Union, Florence Dunn, president.

He picked up the phone and called Miss Dunn and made an appointment for the same day. The pressure had been building up all morning. He'd seen many newspaper articles and television reports about teachers getting arrested. Fear lodged deep in his gut. It could happen to him. He needed to let someone know about this, someone who could help him deal with it.

He drove to Portsmith and arrived at Dunn's office early.

"Come on in." She directed him to a big, comfortable chair in her office. "You're a teacher at what school?"

"Vista Terrace."

"And what can I do for you?"

Kelvin froze. The tension of the accusation, the anxiety of not knowing the outcome, and the fear of what could happen to him came tumbling down. He burst into tears.

Florence handed him a box of tissues. "Take your time," she said.

He composed himself. He blew his nose with the tissues and wiped his eyes. "On Monday, I was called into the office. Someone named Prudence Hall told me a sixth grade student accused me of molesting them."

"Boy or a girl?"

"Girl."

"Okay, then what happened?"

"I was placed on administrative leave."

"Have you spoken to anyone else about this?"

"Yes, a detective came to my house yesterday."

"And you spoke to him?" Florence asked.

"Yes."

"With or without an attorney present?"

"Without."

"Arrrrrrgh!" Florence dropped her head down. After a moment, she lifted it up. "You never speak to anyone without an attorney. I'll get you one."

"I don't need an attorney," Kelvin said.

"Yes, you do!" Florence shrieked. She picked up the phone and pressed a button. After a short pause, "It's Florence. Call me back. I've got someone who needs to see you ASAP." She put the phone down. "So, who came to see you?"

"I believe his name was Detective Washington."

"Portsmith police?"

"Yes."

"Okay, you gotta talk to Gerry Daily as soon as you can. I'm going to write down his name and number. He's the union's attorney. I left him a message, but I'd like you to follow up with a call as well. We cover the costs."

"I'm not sure if I'm a member. I remember filling something out at the new hires orientation."

"That's okay. I'm still going to cover you. I'll give you a membership application. If you're not a member, you can join as soon as you're off administrative leave."

"How long will that take?"

"It's different in every case."

"You've had teachers on administrative leave before?" Kelvin asked.

"Yes." Florence handed him a piece of paper. "But it's usually for inappropriate corporal punishment."

"What's that?"

"That's when a student says a teacher hit them. It's quite common."

"Have you had any teacher accused of molestation before?"

Florence paused. "No, not that I can recall."

"Have teachers who are placed on administrative leave been allowed to return to work?"

"Yes, of course. Once the investigation clears you, you'll be allowed back."

"Without prejudice?"

"What do you mean?"

"They're not going to change my assignment or anything?"

Florence sighed. "It's hard to say. They can't legally discriminate against you for being cleared of a crime. People will have their own opinions, and they will talk. There's nothing you can do about that. But if someone says anything you regard as libelous, let me know and I can deal with that."

"Thank you," Kelvin said.

"The important thing now is that you contact Daily. We cover you for the first ten thousand dollars in a criminal case. He's a very good criminal defense attorney." Florence got up from her desk and walked over to a table. She picked up a brochure and handed it to him. "Here's some information about our organization. How did you know to come here?"

"I received a pamphlet at orientation."

"You have my number. Call me if you need anything. But call Daily first."

Kelvin got up and Florence escorted him out. As he walked to his car, he reflected on what she'd said. His mobile phone rang. He looked at it but did not recognize the number. He really didn't want to talk to anyone he didn't know at this point, so he didn't answer.

**

Lara slammed down the receiver. Amazingly, Portsmith still had a working payphone. She didn't dare call Kelvin from the school phone because those calls could be monitored, so she'd slipped out to use the phone at the corner store.

What made it so frustrating was that there was no number for him to call her back. She had to get to the phone store and have her mobile replaced. Lara made a mental note to do that first thing after school.

For the first time in two days, she straightened her shoulders and lifted her chin. Logan's revelation cleared Kelvin. It had to have been someone else. Lara hurried from the store to get back to work.

The climate at the school was chilly. People whispered behind closed doors about Kelvin. No one said anything to her directly. She hoped the staff respected discretion. Although uncomfortable, she went through the motions of doing her job with a clearer head and no pounding temples.

The day passed without incident. She waited for law enforcement to question her so she could confirm Kelvin's whereabouts during fourth period on Monday, but they didn't come back. Apparently, they'd been at the school the previous day, when she'd been absent.

What had he told them? Did he dare mention the book room? Had he been briefed as to what time the alleged incident happened? Her stomach was in knots and her palms perspired. She had to speak to Kelvin before she spoke to anyone else.

Lara left shortly after dismissal. She didn't even check in with Miss Hawthorne. She headed straight home and picked up the pieces of her broken phone off the floor, placed them a plastic bag, and headed back out the door.

Fortunately, she didn't have to drive far to find a phone store. Since she'd left work at a reasonable hour, she made it to the store long before closing time. The courteous sales associate managed to save the day and set her up with a new phone.

Outside the store, she got into her car and immediately called Kelvin. He answered on the first ring.

"Lara…"

"Kelvin, listen to me. The student said it happened fourth period Monday. You were with me the whole time. Who did you tell?"

"No one."

"Whom have you spoken to?"

"A police detective."

"And you didn't tell him?"

"I didn't know the accusation was fourth period. No one ever told me when."

"Okay, then we need to tell someone right away, Kelvin."

"I have an appointment with an attorney tomorrow."

"Who?"

"Someone named Daily. The union set it up."

Lara sighed. "So you told the teachers' union?"

"Yes, I had to talk to someone."

"That's good. You need someone on your side. I've heard of Daily. You can see his face on billboards all over town. I'm going with you to your appointment. What time is it?"

"Four o'clock."

"I'll meet you there."

"You have the address?"

"I'll look it up when I get home. I'm in my car now. See you tomorrow."

Kelvin's voice made her heart surge. She hoped all of this would be over soon. The man she'd grown so dangerously attracted to had to be innocent. The warmth in her core betrayed her desire for him.

She placed her phone in her handbag and started the engine. Four o'clock tomorrow seemed like a long time from now.

This had to be a false accusation and nothing more. She'd have to expose what she and Kelvin were doing fourth period Monday in the book room. No point in hiding it, because anyone could have walked by and heard them. They'd both be fired, but she didn't care. The damn job was a nightmare of pressure, and Vista Terrace had a toxic atmosphere.

She had to get this off of her mind for now. When she got home, she called Cassie, whom she hadn't seen since the summer. She needed a night out of food and drink. Maybe see a film for escapism. Something to forget Vista Terrace.

Cassie could be considered Lara's alter ego. They'd attended high school together but navigated different paths after graduation. In many ways, they were very much alike. Lara had taken the college/professional track while Cassie had gone to cosmetology school. Some, including those in her family, had looked down on her at the time. Today, she owned her own salon.

"It's about time!" Cassie said. She greeted Lara with a big smile and a bigger hug. Cassie had flaming red hair. It almost looked as though it were on fire. She also dressed retro, like someone out of an eighties movie.

"I know…I work too much." Lara had let Cassie select

the place. Nicolodi's Italian Bistro, and Lara planned to pick the movie if they decided to see one later.

"How's the new job?"

Lara rolled her eyes. "Too early to tell. You know, beginning of the year adjustments and all that."

A server placed some bruschetta on their table and handed Cassie a wine list. She gave it a glance and then turned to Lara.

"The Chianti is quite good here."

"Chianti it is," Lara said.

Cassie handed the wine list back to the server.

"I'll take anything at this point." Lara twisted her napkin.

"That kind of a week already?"

"That's public education. Enough about me, how have you been doing?"

"Great! Keeping busy. The salon is doing really well."

"That's good to hear. You've accomplished a great deal for yourself."

Cassie smiled broadly. "I keep telling myself that, too. Some day I'll believe it."

Lara bit into the bruschetta, but she couldn't take her mind off the trouble at Vista Terrace

"Is it that bad?"

She wasn't sure how to answer. "It'll get better."

"Is it more than just the job?"

Fighting back the moisture that welled in her eyes, she couldn't say anything, so she just nodded.

"A man." Cassie didn't say it as though it were a question.

Lara didn't respond right away. "It's complicated."

"They all are," Cassie quipped.

"You know I haven't had the best luck with men."

"That's because you never really made it a priority in your life. Is it now?"

Lara shook her head. "I don't know. There hasn't been enough time to say."

"Is it someone from school?"

"Yes."

"I guess that complicates things."

"More than you know," Lara said softly.

The server arrived with a bottle of Chianti. "It's fine." Cassie waved him away without tasting it. "So, tell me about him."

"I'd rather not discuss him tonight. I need some time to not think about any of the new stuff in my life, work or Kelvin."

"Kelvin… as in Kelvin Young?"

Lara rolled her eyes. "Shit, I didn't mean to say his name."

"You're dating Kelvin Young?" Cassie's eyes looked like saucers.

"Well, it was just one or two dates."

"Daaaaaayuuuuuum and a half! How the hell did you ever meet Kelvin Young?"

"Chance encounter."

"Is he every bit as awesome—"

"Cassie, you know I'm not good with men."

"Lara, if there was ever a time to get over it, this is the time."

Lara looked away.

"I'm sorry," Cassie said. "I didn't mean to be insensitive. But with Luke put away…"

"Yeah. For something he did to someone else. Not me."

"Does it matter as long as he's paying the price?"

"Can we talk about something else?"

"Yes. Kelvin Young. I want to hear all about him."

"Tonight's not the night." Lara reached for her glass. "Tonight's the night to have fun."

"Have you fallen for him?"

She avoided looking directly at Cassie. Of course Lara had fallen for him. She couldn't have had the violent reaction she had in the bathroom if she hadn't fallen for him. He was attentive, well bred, and had a big heart. Being with him was a dream. He could talk to and treat a woman right.

And he's a suspect in a criminal investigation.

CHAPTER SIXTEEN

Thursday dragged on forever. Kelvin's appointment with Gerry Daily wasn't until four o'clock. Restless, Kelvin drove up to Portsmith early. He spent some time wandering around one of the huge chain stores on the edge of town. He found it odd to be in a store in the middle of a school day. His place was in the classroom teaching. He meandered slowly around the store until he found the book section and browsed through some paperbacks to pass the time.

"Coach."

He instinctively looked up, a wave of panic running through him. A broad-shouldered man was looking at him.

"You are a coach, right?"

He nodded.

"I think we've met before. Dr. Hamilton introduced us. Devon Jackson." He extended his hand.

Kelvin shook it. "Yes, I remember now. You're also a coach and you teach math."

"That's right. High school. I'm sorry, I don't remember your name."

"Kelvin."

"I guess we're both playing hooky today. I just needed a day off to do some personal errands, you know?"

Mr. Jackson shifted his weight from one foot to the other and didn't maintain eye contact.

"Yeah…same here."

"Funny we picked the same day." Jackson laughed.

Kelvin found it odd. He certainly wasn't expecting to see a teacher shopping in the middle of a school day.

"How's your team doing?" Jackson asked.

"Great. They're a fine group of boys."

"Yeah, mine are awesome as well. Good to see you, Coach." Jackson made the peace sign and scurried away.

Kelvin stared at him for a moment.

What's he really doing here?

Strange. Mr. Jackson was a math teacher and football coach. The school year was just beginning. It seemed odd to take a day off for personal errands so early in the year.

He was also one of Dr. Hamilton's hires.

Are we all targets?

An odd tingling sensation crept up his neck. Something wasn't right here. Jackson seemed to be making excuses for why he'd taken the day off. Perhaps it wasn't voluntary.

Can he be on administrative leave?

He shook his head. It was a crazy thought. Yet, in some bizarre way, it made sense right now. He put down the paperback.

Kelvin arrived at Gerry Daily's office early. The receptionist offered him something to drink, but he declined. He sat in the reception area. This was the first time in his life he was in the office of a criminal defense attorney. It was a modest brick building on the outside, located on a street in town that got plenty of traffic.

A few minutes before four, Lara walked in. She sat next to Kelvin without a word.

She's uncomfortable around me.

"Good afternoon. I'm Gerry Daily." Kelvin immediately recognized his face from the billboards, and stood to shake his hand. "Kelvin Young. This is one of my co-workers, Lara Rumson."

"Good to meet you both. Please follow me."

Daily led them into a conference room. It looked like what a law office conference room should look like. Walls lined with books, big, shiny, round table, and large leather chairs.

"Please, sit down. Did Paula offer you anything to drink?"

Kelvin glanced at Lara.

"Nothing for me, thanks," Lara said.

Daily pulled out a legal pad, and Kelvin repeated his story, starting with being called into Hawthorne's office, and ending with Florence Dunn.

"He never showed you his badge." Daily chuckled. "Wow, that's a first for me. What did you say his name was?" Daily glanced down at his notes.

"Washington," Kelvin said.

"Oh, yeah, I see it here."

Kelvin handed Daily the detective's business card. "Here's the card he gave me."

With a squint, Daily stared at the card and burst out laughing. "Oh, no, he didn't. He doesn't even have his own card? This is a riot."

Daily turned his attention to Lara. "Do you have anything to add?"

"Yes, I do. On Wednesday, the school counselor told me that the alleged incident took place on Monday during fourth period. I was with Kelvin the entire time."

Daily spread his arms open. "So?"

"He has an alibi."

Daily shook his head and lowered it, as though he was trying not to laugh.

"Miss Rumson, I don't mean to be disrespectful, but you've been watching too much television. Alibis are something you only hear on TV."

"What do you mean?"

"It doesn't mean anything. The prosecutor is just going to say the girl was mistaken about the day or mistaken about the time."

Lara glanced at Kelvin. "What do you mean, the prosecutor?"

"This is how it works. Your detective friend is going to file a report. That report goes to the district attorney. He decides whether or not to bring charges."

"So there's nothing I can do?" Kelvin asked.

"Mr. Young, you haven't been arrested. You haven't been charged with any crime." Daily spread his arms wide.

"So what do I do?"

"You're on administrative leave with pay. Take in a movie, do something to get it off your mind until it gets resolved. The most important thing is that you do not talk to anyone—and I mean anyone. If you are contacted by any law enforcement official, call me immediately. Don't speak to anyone."

Kelvin nodded.

"Here's my card."

**

Out in the parking lot, Kelvin walked Lara to her car.

"I hope that helped. Anything else you want to talk about?" Lara asked.

Kelvin shook his head. "We can't be seen together. We can't go anywhere together until this blows over. It's for your protection."

"What do you mean?"

"He gave me specific instructions to speak to no one, and that especially includes anyone at Vista Terrace."

His words sunk in. She wished they hadn't. "I still can't believe what he said about the alibi."

"That sounds crazy, but I guess he would know."

"I'm not so sure," Lara said. Smelling a rat had become her specialty since working at Vista Terrace.

"What do you mean?"

"The union sent you to him. What has the union really done for you?"

"Sent me to him, I guess."

"Did they explain to you the policies and procedures for placing a teacher on administrative leave?"

"No."

"Did they tell you your rights and responsibilities as a teacher on administrative leave?"

"No."

"Are they advocating to get you off administrative leave to save your name, your career, and your good standing?"

Kelvin shook his head.

"Now you know what to ask at your next meeting with Florence Dunn. I'll be there for that one as well."

She opened her car door and watched Kelvin walk away, dejected. Hopeless to do anything else at this point, she started her engine. Not at all satisfied by the meeting with Daily, she pulled out of the parking lot.

Something smells.

Friday didn't feel like a Friday for Lara. It seemed as though a dark cloud hung over Vista Terrace. The halls were quiet, and people seemed to avoid eye contact with her.

How much do they know?

They whispered behind her back as well, but she didn't care. She wanted to see Kelvin's name cleared. Something didn't feel right on this campus. She had this nagging feeling but couldn't figure out why. The atmosphere permeated every room, and it was uncomfortable getting through the day.

Miss Hawthorne appeared unchanged. She had her eyes on everything. Several times Lara was asked to assist Miss Day with this or assist Miss Day with that. Kelvin's substitute was getting more support than he had gotten.

Lara almost laughed at the irony. How long would this

go on? Hamilton's recruits being treated differently from others. Lara had already decided that if she chose to remain at Vista Terrace next year, she would have to insist on being relocated into a real office. Although, in light of recent events, next year seemed like a long, long time away.

"How's your day going?" Miss Howard stood in the doorway with a tight, closed-lip smile. The art teacher was one of Lara's least favorite people.

"Fine," Lara said.

"Any word?"

"On what?"

"Mr. Young."

"No," Lara said curtly.

"Have you heard from him?"

"No." She had no interest in discussing anything with Miss Howard, nor would she risk giving her any bait for gossip. "I have work to do." She turned slightly so that her back was almost to Miss Howard.

The day dragged on. It was the longest Friday in recent memory. When the dismissal bell rang, she cleaned up her desk and reported to afternoon duty. She did her part to get kids on the buses safely. After the last one rolled out of the lot, she walked to her car. Her weekend had started.

She drove home with a sinking feeling in her stomach. She still had some conflicted feelings about Kelvin. He was innocent of any crime, but there was a question that remained.

Why did the girl accuse Kelvin?

First of all, there was the mother. She clearly had it in for Kelvin. That whole nonsense about having the other daughter moved out of Kelvin's class… Could they be that prejudiced?

Thoughts swirled around her mind. She could almost smell a conspiracy. Things didn't add up. Florence Dunn's only interest was to get him a defense attorney. That would make sense had he been arrested and charged, but he hadn't. She hadn't done anything to challenge the district placing him on administrative leave.

Why hadn't Dunn encouraged Kelvin to challenge the district?

Gerry Daily had told them there was no such thing as an alibi. That was ridiculous. She didn't believe it.

Were they all in cahoots together?

It was a crazy, but with further pondering, it almost made sense. The situation was supposed to remain confidential, yet the looks on their faces indicated that everyone at the school had been talking about it.

How had it leaked?

Kelvin told Daily there had only been three other people in the room: Hawthorne, Hall, and Page.

Which one of them was the least trustworthy?

That was a difficult call. Lara didn't really know Hall and had never even met Page. Hawthorne may have had some obligation to tell the counselor. Miss Logan didn't seem like a gossip, but at Vista Terrace anyone could be one.

Who has something to gain by harming Kelvin?

When Lara arrived at her condo, she had one thing on her mind. Rest. After the dreadful day she'd had, a nap was in order. She climbed into bed and pulled the covers up tight to her neck.

When she finally opened her eyes, it was Saturday

morning. She'd had a restless sleep, waking often. She glanced at the clock. It was just after six a.m. She had slept through the night without eating any dinner.

Lara pulled herself out of bed. It was still dark outside. She needed coffee, and as it brewed, she tried to forget that she'd tossed and turned all night. It was something Daily had said: *The prosecutor is just going to say the girl was mistaken about the day or mistaken about the time.*

What if he was correct? What was it going to take to eliminate that nagging doubt? No wonder she hadn't gotten out of bed last night. This all had become too much pressure on her. She struggled with uncertainty. Her feelings for Kelvin were now overshadowed by doubt. This wasn't healthy.

The weekend they'd spent together was a turning point for Lara. She had met a man who put her at ease, made her feel special and interesting, and brought out her unbridled passion. The time they'd spent together had signaled the start of something grander in her life. Kelvin couldn't be dismissed as a date or a fling. His presence had become so much stronger.

He's a suspect in a criminal investigation.

Could it be some bizarre misunderstanding? Would it clear up soon? Lara couldn't imagine it taking long to investigate. She needed to stop thinking about it but she couldn't. It brought back all these memories of her brother, Luke, and his assaults on her. She could be that young girl crying out an accusation. But when it had happened to Lara, she hadn't done anything or said anything out of fear. Here she was, over a decade later, reliving all of it.

Clamminess enveloped her body as she shuddered. She

closed her eyes and willed the painful memories away. After she wiped her hands with a napkin to absorb the sweat, she opened her eyes and took a few deep breaths.

Why didn't I say something all those years ago?

Lara needed a protein-rich breakfast since she'd had no dinner. She opened the fridge and pulled out a carton of eggs, heated up a skillet, then poured herself a cup of coffee. At the moment, she craved that more than protein.

She had to find something to do to help Kelvin. Brainstorm. Come up with some idea that he could pursue. She supported him but was, at the same time, anxious for the day to come when he'd be cleared. Thinking about all this could drive her mad.

Shopping. Movies. Visit with Mom and Dad. Read a few good romance novels. Reading would probably take her mind off things better than anything else. It was the only activity that kept the brain occupied. Movies were good escapism, but depending on the type of film, it could be too passive an experience to distract her.

Lara was a paperback novel addict. She had shelves full of paperback novels she hadn't read. The covers were what sold her. She'd go to a bookstore, and if the cover looked good, she'd buy the book. Most of the time, she wouldn't even read the blurb on the back cover. Dozens of romance paperbacks with provocative covers filled her bookcase.

After she finished her eggs and toast, she raided her bookcase and pulled a few paperbacks off the shelf. She poured another cup of coffee and found a comfy chair.

Sylvia Day, take me away!

CHAPTER SEVENTEEN

Kelvin had never experienced such boredom and helplessness before. Every day he was on administrative leave was a day he didn't work with his students. That bothered him, gnawed at him, and angered him. So unfair—except this nightmare had become his reality.

The weekend arrived. He was still anxious and had nothing to do. Someone else coaching his boys or a substitute teaching his classes made him mad. And, unfortunately, still powerless to do anything.

He wanted to see Lara but it wasn't wise. It wouldn't be right until this thing had passed. Images of her beautiful face and soft body filled his mind, and he took some comfort in that.

Going to the gym also helped him clear his head, so Kelvin went early Saturday morning. His workout routine gave him focus. Exercise boosted his spirits and fueled his passion. At the gym, he concentrated on building his body.

I miss her.

He had the whole day ahead of him as well as tomorrow.

Nothing in his favor would transpire over the weekend. Perhaps he could call her. If he couldn't see her, he at least wanted to hear her voice.

He'd do anything possible to keep them together. He couldn't imagine what kind of thoughts were running through Lara's mind now. She seemed supportive, and he was grateful she'd attended the meeting with Daily.

On the other hand, she still reported to Vista Terrace every day and potentially listened to a slew of gossip. He had no idea who could influence her. His stomach twisted from fear of losing her.

I need to clear my name.

If he listened to what everyone had said—Dunn, Daily, and Hawthorne—there wasn't anything he could do. That frustrated Kelvin beyond words. There had to be something he could do, some action he could take. He just hadn't figured it out yet.

What if they are all in this together?

He had to run that one by Lara, as she'd implied as much herself after that meeting with Daily. He didn't think it was just his imagination. They all seemed to be telling him the same thing. It was almost scripted.

Kelvin chuckled. It was scripted. Detective Washington had read his Miranda rights from a script. Any school kid could recite that by heart. A seasoned detective would have that memorized.

What if he's an actor hired by Hawthorne or the school district?

Kelvin shook his head. It didn't make any sense. None of

it. Even Daily didn't make any sense saying there was no such thing as an alibi. How could that be? Lara had found that odd as well. None of this added up.

Something else had bothered Kelvin. Something he'd almost said to the police detective but hadn't. Kelvin was smart enough not to volunteer information. Yet it troubled him enough to run it by someone. He searched for Daily's card and dialed his number. Surprisingly, he got an answer.

"Gerry Daily."

"Mr. Daily, this is Kelvin Young."

"What can I do for you?"

"There's something I forgot to mention the other day. There is another black teacher at the school named Mr. Strode. Several of the adults have called me by his name."

"And?"

"If the adults have us confused, isn't it possible some of the children do as well?"

"It's possible," Daily answered. "If that's the case, it will come out in the investigation."

"Do you give the Portsmith police that much credit?"

"Yes, I do, Mr. Young. If there was an attack that took place at the school, every male will be investigated in one way or another. You just took one for the team. Let the investigation run its course."

So I took one for the team?

"Oh, Mr. Young. One more thing. I did a little investigation on your friend Detective Washington. He's legit. Just promoted, that's why he doesn't have his own business card yet. As far as not showing you a badge, did you ask to see it?"

"No."

"Well, there you go."

"So, you don't think they're trying to railroad me?"

"How? Why? There's no evidence of that at all, Mr. Young. I know this seems strange to you, but it is what it is."

Kelvin shook his head. This fiasco was getting more bizarre each day. He ran his hand over his face. He still hadn't told his parents what was going on. Since it hadn't hit the news, he'd had no compulsion to tell them. With nothing but time on his hands, he had to let them know.

He drove over to his parents' house, a grand estate on a huge piece of land. He'd grown up in this house, filled with memories of hearty southern cooking and plenty of room to run around and get lost with his brother, Malik. For the first time since this drama had started, his body loosened a bit. Some of the tension melted away at the sight of his childhood home.

He arrived, and the maid led him to his parents having their evening coffee in the parlor. The room featured overstuffed sofas and framed photographs displayed on small round tables.

His parents always greeted Kelvin with a smile.

After the pleasantries, Kelvin began, "I'm glad you're both in the same room so I don't have to tell the story twice." He let out a nervous laugh and told them the whole story.

"I knew it," his mother said. "I always knew something like this would happen if you went up there." With a linen napkin draped over her skirt, she placed her cup on its saucer. Her swept up salt and pepper hair glistened with hairspray. Mrs. Young always looked her finest.

"Up where?"

"Portsmith. You were doing fine here."

"I was recruited."

"Recruited, yes." His father placed his coffee cup down. "Not drafted. You could have turned down the offer." He always wore a suit. A tall man, taller than Kelvin, Mr. Young's sharp words resonated.

Kelvin could barely speak.

His mother shook her head. "We don't mean to sound like you're to blame for this."

"No, you've done nothing wrong. We're just saying Portsmith isn't exactly the place for a Young."

His mother nodded. "Your father is right. In a place like that, you just call attention to yourself. You're a target."

"You think the girl made that accusation because I'm a Young?"

"Of course," his father said. "The civil suit will follow. They just want money. Why else would anyone say that kind of rubbish?"

Kelvin sank deeper into the couch. He hated to admit it, but his parents' words made some sense.

**

The weekend had dragged on forever for Lara. She'd finished a few good books, but the conflicting feelings about Kelvin were like a bad itch in a place she couldn't scratch.

When Monday morning came, she had work to keep her busy. Never before had she been grateful to go to Vista Terrace. She dived into it and offered help in several classrooms. She occupied her mind as much as possible hoping the day would go by quicker.

During fourth period, she tried to catch up on some work at her desk. "Hello, Mizz Rumson. Can you help me with something?" Lewis asked. "One of the science teachers asked me for something out of the supply closet. I don't want to bring her the wrong thing. Graduate…"

"Graduated cylinder. Sure." She got up from her desk. "Why are they in a supply closet and not in the classroom?"

"Theft. Mizz Hawthorne says too much stuff disappears from this place. She don't give anyone the key if she can help it. I've got a key. Maybe one other person on campus if I remember right."

"It's not on my giant key ring?"

"No, ma'am. No disrespect to you, but Mizz Hawthorne wouldn't give that key to a newcomer, as far as I know."

"Fine, let's go."

"We don't really use that closet for much of anything but the expensive stuff."

Lewis led Lara down the maze of corridors in the school. They finally came to a remote wing near the back of the building. Special Education was dumped back here, and it was rare for anyone to venture to the wing.

Lewis fumbled with the key to the storage room and opened the door for Lara. With one hand, Lara clutched onto Lewis's arm for strength and clamped the other hand over her mouth to suppress a scream.

CHAPTER EIGHTEEN

Kelvin sat passively on his couch. He flipped through channels, not really focusing on anything. He caught the tail end of a teaser for the news. A picture of Randy Strode flashed onto the screen. He gripped the remote and jacked up the volume.

Incredible.

He couldn't believe what he was seeing. Yet it made perfect sense. In fact, it was the only thing in this bizarre nightmare that made any sense at all. Strode was aloof, sneaky, and often not in his room when he was supposed to be. He'd been arrested whereas Kelvin had not been.

That means something happened.

Kelvin grabbed for his phone but had no idea whom he should call. Dunn? Daily? Lara? He decided on Daily and explained what he'd seen on the news.

"It sounds like good news for you, but realistically speaking, nothing is going to happen unless the police can make a connection between Strode and your accuser. You're just going to have to wait, Mr. Young. There's nothing you can do about it."

There's nothing you can do about it.

How many times had that phrase been tossed out since Kelvin had arrived in Portsmith? It seemed to be how people lived their lives here. It grew tiresome.

With his heart racing, he called Lara but didn't get an answer. He left her a short voice mail. There had to be something she could tell him that would be in his favor.

You're just going to have to wait, Mr. Young.

The past week had seemed like an eternity. Every morning he'd woken up expecting the phone to ring with a message telling him it was all a mistake. He'd risen at his regular time every day so he would be prepared when the call came. He'd even dressed for work, certain this misunderstanding would blow over soon.

Maybe Lara would call him back. Being at the school all day, she would probably have more details than the news. Daily had said there was nothing he could do but wait. Kelvin wasn't good at waiting—it frustrated him. His chest tightened and a dull ache permeated through his head.

How is Lara holding up?

He wanted to give her a strong hug and tell her how much he cared. She deserved stability in her life, and right now he couldn't offer that. His life was in limbo until he could be taken off administrative leave. As much as he fought it, perhaps there really was nothing he could do about it.

Will Lara be able to move past this?

It was too early to say. The situation hadn't resolved, but he remained hopeful. This business with Strode getting arrested must mean something. If only he could talk to Lara. He needed to communicate to her how seriously he valued their friendship. It was more than friendship, but every strong relationship grew from a friendship.

He went to sleep and woke up Tuesday morning still thinking of Lara. She hadn't returned his call from last night. It must have had something to do with the Strode case. Perhaps no one on campus had permission to speak about it.

Like with me.

Before heading to the gym, he searched online for any articles on Strode. They repeated most of the information he'd already gotten from the news, plus one important fact. The allegations were corroborated by two adult witnesses.

Two adult witnesses.

Kelvin's heartbeat surged. Who could they be? Kelvin called Lara again, but the call went to voice mail. Perhaps she wasn't allowed to speak to him.

She couldn't answer her mobile phone at work. That wasn't unusual. And it probably wouldn't help to call Dunn at this point in light of what Daily had said. Kelvin found the whole situation maddening. Something was going on at that school, and his name had been dragged into it. Thankfully, it hadn't gone public as it had with Strode's.

Kelvin couldn't think of anyone else to call. He had to get his mind off this somehow.

**

Chaotic described Tuesday at Vista Terrace. The wing with the storage closet was closed off with police tape. Those classes, which were Special Ed, had to be relocated to the library, gymnasium, or wherever they could fit. Strode's room was taped off and his computer confiscated. His classes were held in the auditorium. No substitute showed up, so Lara, Miss Logan, and the librarian had to hold his classes. Lara didn't mind because it kept her busy and focused on serving the needs of children. Miss Logan stepped up and did her part.

The librarian whined to Lara: "I work for a school district that's so inept at hiring subs that I have to hold classes. When do I do my own job?"

"Miss Hawthorne would be happy to hear your concerns," Lara said with a sweet smile.

She wasn't surprised no one had picked up the sub opening this morning. With Portsmith being such a small town, everyone had heard about or seen Strode and Vista Terrace on the news. Lara discovered that holding classes made the day race by. She was certainly grateful for that.

A dark and gloomy atmosphere hung over the school, as though no one wanted to be there anymore. Lewis, on the way in, didn't look her in the eye and barely spoke. Lara suspected he was haunted by what he'd seen, and she'd had nightmares about it. Perhaps either he'd known something or he'd suspected something. Maybe that was why he'd led her to that closet.

Either way, it wasn't her problem. The police dealt with that. Poor Lewis. What a predicament to be in. What had he seen or heard before he'd come to her that day?

She wanted to speak to Kelvin, but she remained plagued

with uncertainty. The taint of accusation was a stain not easily erased. The small percentage of lingering doubt could spread like cancer.

The investigation hadn't concluded yet, so she had to be careful not to get involved until the detectives had finished their job. Her day was filled with back-to-back classes, so she'd have no time to see how he was doing until the evening. She still wasn't sure she should call him at all. Now that she was a witness, she had to be cautious.

Lara held one of Strode's classes in the auditorium. They were doing some bookwork when Hawthorne came through with a parade of suits. Lara didn't recognize them immediately, so she wasn't certain if they were detectives or administrators from central office.

"This is my vice-principal, Ms. Lara Rumson. She's agreed to hold classes during our time of need," Miss Hawthorne said to the group.

Agreed? I had no choice.

"This is her first year as an administrator."

Sure, let everyone know I'm a novice.

"We're pleased to have her here at Vista Terrace."

We?

Hawthorne led the gentlemen onward. Lara surmised they must be central administration suits. Hawthorne was doing the look-how-great-my-school-is dance that Lara had seen before.

The school swarmed with suits because of what had happened here—or allegedly happened. Central office probably put a great deal of pressure on Hawthorne to run a tight ship. It would be interesting to hear what the investigation revealed.

**

That evening, Kelvin checked his school email account. He received an email from Prudence Hall instructing him to call her secretary to make an appointment to see her. This had to be good news. Or was he being terminated? School districts hated bad publicity. Was he being dragged down with Strode?

Kelvin glanced at the clock. He'd call in the morning. Meanwhile, he tried calling Lara again. This time she answered.

"Can you talk?" he asked.

"Not really, Kelvin. They don't want us speaking to anyone."

"I figured as much after I saw Strode on the news."

She went silent for a moment.

"You there?"

"Yeah, Kelvin. I'm here. How are you doing?"

"Hangin' in there. Look, I got one bit of news. Prudence Hall sent me an email telling me to call her secretary and set up an appointment."

"Take Dunn with you."

"Why?"

"Kelvin, you need someone by your side. When's your meeting?"

"I don't know. I just read the email. I'm going to call tomorrow."

"After you set up the appointment, call Florence Dunn.

Ask her to go with you. Got it?"

"Got it. How are you doing?"

"Still breathing. This hasn't been a good week."

"I understand if you can't talk about it."

"I can't. We'll talk later, Kelvin. Let me know how your meeting goes."

Kelvin put the phone down. At least he had a plan for the morning. Now he just had to make it through the night.

The next morning, at 8:05 a.m., he called central office and made an appointment to see Prudence Hall the end of the day Friday. Then, he called Florence Dunn and she agreed to go with him.

The week dragged along for Kelvin. He respected Lara's privacy and whatever confidentiality she was bound by, so he didn't call her again—that could wait until Friday.

CHAPTER NINETEEN

When Friday finally rolled around, Kelvin arrived at his appointment early. He waited for Florence Dunn, and they were ushered in to see Prudence Hall.

She rose and shook their hands. "Mr. Young. Oh, I wasn't expecting to see you, Florence."

Florence smiled.

Miss Hall gestured to the woman seated next to her. "This is Alberta Wayne. She's our internal investigator. She's been working closely with the detectives involved with the accusations at Vista Terrace."

"We've met," Florence said.

Kelvin shook Ms. Wayne's hand. Did the Portsmith Independent School District only hire women with archaic names?

"I'm going to let Ms. Wayne do most of the talking since she has the details," Hall said.

Alberta Wayne began reading from a report. "A sixth grade minor child at Vista Terrace Middle School made a criminal accusation against a Mr. Kelvin Young. Mr. Young was immediately placed on administrative leave with pay pending the outcome of an investigation. Detective Darryl Washington of the Portsmith Police Department interviewed Mr. Young. Detective Washington reported that Mr. Young cooperated with the investigation. One week after the accusation was made, two adults at Vista Terrace, Lara Rumson and Lewis Cramer, observed inappropriate behavior between Mr. Randy Strode and a minor child."

Kelvin's stomach turned.

"Subsequently, the sixth grade minor child who made the accusation against Mr. Young was shown a photo lineup of six African-American males. All African-American males employed at Vista Terrace were included in the lineup. The minor child identified a photograph of Mr. Randy Strode as her attacker. She repeatedly referred to him as "Mr. Young" even though she pointed to Randy Strode's picture several times. She made a positive identification that Randy Strode was her attacker. The district attorney's office has declined to press any charges against Mr. Kelvin Young and considers him to be exonerated."

"Well, that's good news for you." Florence squeezed Kelvin's shoulder. "What's going to happen to Strode?"

"We can't comment on that," Ms. Hall said.

"So Mr. Young can go back to work?" Florence asked.

Miss Hall addressed him. "Yes, Mr. Young. You can return to work on Monday."

"Without prejudice?" Dunn asked.

"What do you mean?"

"No one's gonna say, hey, that's the guy!"

"No one knows, Miss Dunn. Miss Hawthorne does an excellent job of maintaining confidentiality." Miss Hall spoke to Kelvin again. "Miss Hawthorne spoke very highly of you, Mr. Young. She believes you're a strong teacher and a benefit to the school."

Kelvin nodded. It was as though the weight of the world had been lifted from his shoulders. Finally, he could return to his students. He wanted nothing more than to forget this nightmare and put it squarely behind him. That day he'd been waiting for had arrived.

"Those children need you," Dunn added.

When Kelvin returned to his car, he immediately called Lara. "I'll be seeing you on Monday. I've been taken off administrative leave. I get to go back to work."

"Kelvin, that's great, but I won't be seeing you on Monday."

"What's wrong?"

"I've been served with a subpoena to testify before a grand jury on Monday."

Kelvin was silent for a moment. "Does that mean I can't see you until after?"

"Under the circumstances, that would be best. I'm sorry, Kelvin. I'm happy for your good news. I'm just not in the best of moods right now."

"I understand. Can I see you when this is over?"

"I hope so. I want this to be over with."

If Kelvin could spend the weekend with Lara, he could take her mind off of everything. But he had to look at it from her perspective. If the defense attorney found out she was spending time with him, it could be held against her. If Strode had an attorney, and he likely did, the attorney would have been in the room when the girl pointed to Strode's picture and identified it as Mr. Young.

He had to stay away from Lara until after her testimony. In light of the strong feelings he'd developed for her, staying away would be hard to do. His days of running around were over. She meant more to him than any woman he'd dated. They were only beginning their journey together when the wrench had gotten thrown in.

With her, he'd found calmness and a contentment that had eluded him all his life. She'd helped him become grounded just by being herself. His cheeks burned from the wild abandonment that had taken place between them. Sometimes, at school.

Kelvin faced a lonely Friday night. Relieved to be off administrative leave, he should have been elated. This nightmare could finally be put to rest. Instead, all he could think about was Lara, so isolated right now. He wanted to see her and hold her, but he had to be patient. Hopefully, Monday would come and go and that would finally be the end of it.

The swelling in his groin was a testament to his impatience. His chest tightened, and he didn't want to wait any longer. She did so much for him.

He owned his own home and enjoyed a career he loved. He was thirty-one, single, and looking toward the future. He wanted Lara to be a part of his future. Communication had never been one of his strong points. Had he said enough? He had to make her understand what he wanted and how much she enriched his life.

Two weeks ago, they had shared a weekend together. The past two weeks, they'd both gotten sucked into a nightmare. That weekend they'd shared was the start of something bigger. He'd wanted their relationship to grow from there. Instead, it'd come to a screeching halt. The frustration tore him up. But he did have something to look forward to—returning to Vista Terrace.

When Monday morning rolled around, he drove up to the school and hoped for a good day.

"The devil is a liar!" one of the office ladies said to him.

"Mr. Young, there are no words," said another.

The words of his co-workers were clearly supportive, but it was obvious everyone had gossiped. His long two weeks in exile had come to an end. Kelvin's students were excited to see him back. He was equally enthused to see them. He loved his career.

The Cartwright girl was gone. Not just from his class but from the school entirely. The parent had withdrawn both girls and enrolled them elsewhere. Probably in a charter school.

The only one he couldn't read was Hawthorne. Although she smiled, her gaze was anything but warm. She eyed him in a manner that made him look over his shoulder the remainder of the day.

**

Lara's weekend had passed like a sloth moving across a highway. Nothing happened. She'd been mentally exhausted and barely left her condo. That gave her plenty of time to reflect.

Girl meets boy. Boy fucks girl. Boy becomes suspect in criminal investigation.

Wow. What a life.

When she'd told Cassie, the response was to head for the hills. She'd gone so far as to say that Lara should abandoned Portsmith ISD altogether and go back to her old district as a classroom teacher.

With my tail between my legs.

Lara wasn't having it. She'd worked too damned hard on her admin certification, and she wasn't about to give it up. Even over the drama at Vista Terrace.

Kelvin had been nothing less than a gentleman with her. Kind. A bit aggressive sexually, but that hadn't turned out to be such a bad thing. It'd brought Lara to a point where she should be—a passionate woman in touch with her sexuality.

The fire that seared her core when she was with him had no precedent. When they were together, an undeniable connection was present. The desire between them had grown to something unstoppable. She had to see this through.

But she also had to accept the consequences. The man she chose to be with could impact her career. And she'd have to live with the fact that folks would be whispering behind his back. Probably for years.

She reported to the court as instructed Monday morning. She had to wait a considerable time before being called. Finally, she answered their questions and left. That was it.

She hated reliving that all over again, but at least now it appeared to be behind her. If it did go to trial, she'd cross that bridge when she came to it.

She glanced at her watch on the way out of court. Too early to call Kelvin—he'd still be at school. Right now she needed food. She'd been too nervous to eat anything this morning.

Marvin's Deli, a little place outside of downtown, stood quiet and nearly empty. She ate a peaceful lunch and tried to forget the drama of the last two weeks.

Time to move forward.

She wasn't jumping up and down with excitement about going back to Vista Terrace.

When she arrived at her condo, Lara pulled a bottle of wine from the fridge and poured a glass. She needed to relax. Mentally, she was exhausted. Middle school would have been dismissed by now, so she called Kelvin.

"Can I come over?" he asked.

"Sure." He would probably be filled with questions, and she preferred to see him in person. She missed him. Kelvin had walked into her life and fulfilled a need she hadn't known she had. He operated so smoothly and effortlessly. That same quality was what made him so right for her. He always made her feel completely safe, as though he was meant to be there.

Then why am I still conflicted?

She tried to shake the feeling. He would be here soon. She hadn't seen him since that brief meeting in Daily's office. Kelvin must have a lot on his mind.

I sure do.

She went to the bathroom to freshen up. It had been a long day and it was still only late afternoon. She had enough time for a quick shower before he arrived. It would also help her relax. The hot water was awesome, even on a hot day. Steam covered the mirrors. She dressed in the bedroom and chose an old top and some worn jeans. No mood to get dolled up.

Her wineglass remained where she'd left it. Before she could decide whether to finish it or not, Kelvin arrived. As soon as he walked through the door, he embraced her. His strong arms held her close to him.

"It's good to see you." Kelvin's words were muffled in the nape of her neck.

"It's good to be seen." Lara held up her empty glass and Kelvin nodded. After pouring them both some wine, she sat down on the couch sideways so she could face him, one knee bent across the cushion and the other leg dangling to the ground.

"How was your day?"

He grinned. "Better than expected. I was welcomed back with open arms. Of course, everyone knew."

She nodded.

"It was great to see my kids, though. Even though I've only known them a short time, I really missed them. How was your day?"

"I got through it." There really wasn't much to say. She'd done her duty and that was it.

"It must have been difficult."

"I just want it to be behind me now. I can't really talk about it anyway."

"Understood."

"So, Kelvin, what do you think? Was it all a vast Portsmith ISD conspiracy?"

He shrugged. "I have no idea. I thought that at first. Maybe to discredit everyone that Hamilton hired. But Daily doesn't think so. He said the detective is legit. So I guess the answer is no."

She nodded. "Strange place we ended up. Portsmith ISD is so shady."

"Will you stay?"

Lara nodded. "I'm not a quitter."

"Good answer. Neither am I." Kelvin exhaled. "Are you hungry?"

"No, I had a late lunch. Are you?"

"No, not really. I just wanted to see you."

The seriousness of his tone made Lara look into his eyes. She couldn't imagine what he must have gone through. His good name had been dragged into the gutter. Thankfully, not publicly, just among all of his co-workers. Now that Strode was facing charges, Kelvin's allegation would hopefully be forgotten.

"I want to put this all behind us, too," he said. "I want us to be able to move forward."

"In what way?"

"I want to be with you." He took her hand.

He wants to be with me. Am I ready to be with him?

It was about time she admitted it to herself. Yes, she was

ready. Years of school and work had taken their toll on her social life. Friends told her she worked too much. Family noticed she appeared preoccupied with schoolwork. Perhaps now was the time for a man.

Kelvin was one hundred and ten percent man. He had an insatiable appetite for making love. She had had no idea she could be so responsive to a man until she'd met him. He stimulated yearnings deep, deep within her.

"I don't know what to say. This school year has been a whirlwind of activity. I enjoy your company, I know that much." The soothing effect he had was better than any bubble bath. Mesmerized by his presence, she had to trust him. For the first time in her life, she needed to trust a man.

"Are you still concerned about the allegations?"

"Not so much. I'm able to let go of that little by little. After today, it should be better. Besides, it wasn't just the allegations."

"Oh?"

There was concern in his voice. "Nothing about you. My own demons. Long suppressed demons. I had some… issues… with an older brother. Something I should have resolved a long time ago." A jitter ran through her, as it did each time she recalled that part of her life. But with Kelvin here, she could let go of that a bit more, too.

"What about now?"

She shrugged. "Perhaps. I've been so focused on just getting past today."

"Should I come back tomorrow?"

Lara laughed. "I wanted to see you. But maybe a night's

sleep is all I need to wash away the remnants of today's testimony."

"I hope so. I don't want to see you stressed about anything. Vista Terrace comes with enough stress."

"Funny, I was almost getting used to it."

Or, at least, accepting it.

"Hawthorne smiled at me but still gave me that wary look."

"That's interesting you should say that. She put on a show of almost complementing me in front of some suits last week."

Kelvin squeezed her hand. She looked at his large charcoal fingers interlaced with her slender peach ones. The contrast was beautiful.

"I want to make a commitment."

"How so?"

"I don't want to see anyone but you. I haven't been involved with anyone seriously in a long time. Perhaps I had my own fears. But I'm ready now."

Am I ready for this?

She tried to imagine herself without him in her life. It wasn't a happy thought. Kelvin clearly filled a need in her. "That does make it easy since I'm certainly not seeing anyone else."

"I hope I'm not making you too uncomfortable, springing this on you after the day you had."

"My thoughts are a little clouded by the day, I'll agree with that. Still, I'm glad you're here."

"Good," he said. "I'd like to keep you glad."

"So much is running through my mind. I've always been such a private, independent person. I guess you could say I've never really let anyone in. Perhaps I did once, during my first year of college. And here I am now, twenty-seven and single."

"Are you single?"

She smiled. Then her smiled turned into a nervous giggle. "I don't know."

"Do you want to be single?"

Lara paused for a moment, her tone serious. "Not when I'm sitting in the same room with you. You've done a lot for me."

"I appreciate you saying so."

"Maybe I'm not the best at expressing myself verbally."

Kelvin shook his head. "You express yourself in so many other ways it doesn't matter. I know you care."

Lara marveled at his confidence. If she could choose one reason she was so drawn to him, it would have to be his confidence. She loved that about him. That quality made her want to be with him.

When she looked into his eyes, the past melted away. Her ears warmed and her belly tingled. The man had charisma, and he made her look toward the future.

"What else do you know?" she asked.

"I know you're beautiful, resilient, and irresistible to me. I know I want you to trust me and allow me to shower you with attention. Can you handle that?"

"Do you see me running away?"

He reached for his glass. "No. If you do, I'm pretty adept at chasing."

"No doubt." Lara wanted to be with him. Sitting here next to him now, she was certain of it. She desired him and wanted to continue the awakening he'd unleashed. Her body surged with heat from his touch, but he also brought a comfort she hadn't known.

"I love you, Lara." Kelvin took her in his arms and kissed her.

She put her arms around his neck and that familiar warmth radiated through her body. The stress of the day, and of the past several weeks, melted away. She'd met the man of her dreams. She trusted Kelvin, and he was right for her. She accepted his love and refused to give in to any lingering bad memories of the past two weeks. They'd spent enough time together for Lara to know she had found the happiness she'd been searching for.

As she held him close to her, the euphoria spread through her. She closed her eyes and surrendered to happiness. The endorphin rush pinged through her and she became light-headed. She didn't care about what anyone else thought, the potential harm to her career, or anything else. She'd see this through and make it work.

She inhaled his masculine scent and gripped his firm, muscular back. Finally, she'd found the man who propelled her out of the darkness of her past. With Kelvin, she could see a future and embrace it.

They didn't move from the couch for the rest of the night.

EPILOGUE

Lara faced her dad, her hands clasped together. "Do I look okay? It's important that I look okay."

"You look beautiful." Her father beamed.

Lara had announced her engagement to Kelvin in June, and they'd decided on an August wedding. The school year had gone remarkably well for both of them. After the scandal died down, Miss Hawthorne's demeanor had warmed. Lara's utility-closet-turned-office had been vacated, and she'd received a respectable office worthy of a vice-principal.

"Are you ready, Lara?"

The music had started. Her father extended his arm and she took it.

This is really happening.

They entered St. John's Church together and all heads turned. Lara's gaze focused on Kelvin, standing at an altar that seemed miles away. Her father led her up the aisle, and she appreciated his slow pace. Today was a day she'd dreamed her parents would see. Her mother stood proudly in her pew and nodded to Lara. That was her mother's way of communicating that she was doing the right thing.

Kelvin's brother, Malik, served as best man. Lara had asked a few friends to be bridesmaids, Cassie included, but only one who worked at Vista Terrace. She'd chosen Miss Logan, the only person to show her any genuine kindness. She'd become a real friend as the year progressed.

They'd invited Miss Hawthorne, and Lara was pleased to see her in attendance. She sat with Lewis. Lara had developed affection for him over the school year.

Kelvin looked gorgeous in a white tux. He wore studs in his ears, and they caught the light of the candles on the altar. Lara's dress shimmered with white satin and taffeta. Cassie had recommended a designer in Baton Rouge, and Lara couldn't be more satisfied with the gown.

She reached the altar, and he met her with his brilliant smile. He took her hand, and the Catholic priest began the marriage ceremony. She looked into Kelvin's eyes and relished the happiness they'd shared during the past year together.

It's really been a year.

The rocky start had smoothed out into a journey of growth and discovery. Now, Lara could finally say she'd found true happiness. He enriched her life in a way she hadn't imagined possible. Day after day, she took comfort in his gestures of love. He made her happy, and she had a remarkable man for a husband, friend, and lover. He made her so proud to become Mrs. Kelvin Young.

If you enjoyed Kelvin and Lara's story, please consider leaving a review on the retail site where you purchased it, or on Goodreads.

Kelvin and Lara also appear in the novelettes, *A Halloween Treat* and *A Halloween Trick*.

About the author

Jamie Jones writes interracial romance. Jamie spent nine years working as a public school teacher, and that provided the backdrop of Jamie's debut series, The Tempted Teachers Series. *Lesson Plans, Guided Practice,* and *Explicit Instruction* all take place within the framework of the public education system.

Now, Jamie is excited to introduce a new series: The Bennett Family Series. Jamie lives in Austin, Texas....where people are nice.

Visit my website at jamiejonesauthor.com

Also by Jamie Jones

The Tempted Teachers Series

novels
LESSON PLANS (Book 1)
GUIDED PRACTICE (Book 2)
EXPLICIT INSTRUCTION (Book 3)

novellas
RESPONSE TO INTERVENTION (Book 4)
COMMON CORE (Book 5)
PROFESSIONAL DEVELOPMENT (Book 6)
BELL RINGERS (Books 4-6 in one volume)

novelettes
A HALLOWEEN TREAT
A HALLOWEEN TRICK
A CHRISTMAS HONEYMOON
A CHRISTMAS ANNIVERSARY
COMMON CORE: SUMMER SCHOOL
A THANKSGIVING GIFT
EARLY FINISHERS (all six novelettes in one volume)

The Bennett Family Series

Here is a brief excerpt from
Explicit Instruction

Appointments were a pain in the ass. Nikki Dayton didn't make a habit of being on time. It was hot, she was tired, and on top of that she ran late. She'd worked a full shift at the restaurant and had gotten the latest appointment she could with her advisor. Meeting with that woman today was crucial, as she'd procrastinated long enough. Damn, this was when Nikki would get her student teaching assignment. The last major hurdle toward finishing her program and earning her degree.

Her car snaked along the winding road to Arcadia College. She had a four o'clock appointment and the dashboard clock displayed four forty-five. Her advisor would probably blow a gasket if her car didn't first. The old workhorse had served her well since she was sixteen. Five years later, it still sputtered along.

Double shifts at the restaurant had paid for college, and she wasn't about to blow it now. As she maneuvered her car around the last bend, she hoped her advisor would still be there. Then it happened.

The car stopped, and Nikki froze. There wasn't any kind of a pop, so she couldn't have a blow out. Besides, that wouldn't have made the car stop. The engine had cut off. She turned the key in the ignition and nothing happened.

Why does this always happen to me?

She stepped out of her Toyota Camry and walked around the car. Unfortunately, she knew little of cars, so she really didn't know what she was looking for. A few cars passed her but didn't stop. Then again, she hadn't turned on her emergency lights.

Is this an emergency?

Nikki clenched her fists and squinted in the bright Louisiana sunshine. Her advisor probably thought she'd flaked. This assignment meant everything to Nikki, and she was about to be even more delayed.

Damn. Why had she waited so long? By never turning down a shift at the restaurant, that's how. Go to class. Go to work. That had been her routine for several years, going into this fourth and last year.

She kicked a few pebbles and ran a hand through her hair. The air smelled of dust and freshly cut grass. Not the best combination.

That appointment was the key to her future. She'd walk up the damned drive and leave her crappy old junk heap here.

A hip-hop song blasted from somewhere down the road, drowning out any other sounds. Not a new tune, but some OG classic from long ago. Within a hot minute, a shiny, spotless, San Marino Blue BMW crawled to a stop right by her.

"Need a lift?" The young man wore shades concealing his eyes, but he sported a bright smile and a silky voice.

"No," Nikki answered perhaps too quickly. But it was true. She didn't need a lift. She needed help getting her car started.

"What's wrong?"

Nikki frowned. Would she be standing by the road if she could tell him what's wrong? She shrugged.

"Can I take a look?"

Nikki took a look at *him*. A young black man, lean muscular arms, thug brother from the hood kinda look. His smile featured a sparkling gold grill, and he wore a green cap with a matching green and white shirt.

"Sure," Nikki said. She probably would have turned him down had it not been for her advisory appointment.

The sinewy young man stepped out of the car. She could practically catch a whiff the new car smell. He was tall, towering over her. His green and white shorts and matching athletic shoes were perfectly clean. The only thing missing from the image he tried to project was the bling.

"Pop the hood."

Nikki hesitated. Did he figure out she knew nothing of cars? His lanky arm reached through the open window and pulled something. The hood popped open, and he disappeared under it. When Nikki took a few steps towards the front of her vehicle, she was greeted with a view of his perfectly round buttocks.

She shifted her weigh from one foot to the other. Heat surged through her core, and it had nothing to do with the late summer temperature. This wasn't time to think about a young man's buns. What she needed to focus on was the important advisory meeting—a meeting that she missed.

"Found it. You got a wrench?"

Nikki raised her arms, palms up. The young man nodded, went to his car and returned with the needed tool. He was back under the hood for less than a minute before he emerged.

"You're good to go."

He looks so good I'll go with him anywhere.

"What was it?"

"Loose connection on your battery. I tightened it, but you should have a professional look at it next time you take your car in. It'll hold for a while, but it looked corroded so I'd say it needs to be replaced." He hadn't gotten so much of a spot of grease on him. Those designer duds remained pristine.

Nikki nodded. "Thank you."

"You're welcome. Start her up." The young man gestured to her car.

She was the one all started up. A tingling ran through her core and her cheeks burned. But why? He wasn't even remotely her type.

I don't have a type, actually.

Nikki suppressed a smile and got into her car. She turned the key, and it started right up.

"Thanks again." She averted his gaze, certainly she'd blush.

"You're welcome again, miss…"

Nikki waved at him. "I appreciate your help." She stepped on the gas.

He's cute.

He had a sweet smile and the body of an athlete. Well spoken. Well mannered. That contrasted with his manufactured image. Or, perhaps that was his style. But the young man was fine.